Kitchen Sink Gothic
2

Selected by
David A. Riley
and
Linden Riley

Parallel Universe Publications

ISBN: 978-1-9161109-5-3
Parallel Universe Publications, 130 Union Road,
Oswaldtwistle, Lancashire, BB5 3DR, UK

Kitchen Sink Gothic
2

CONTENTS

"I remember saying to myself: 'No more zombies, Joe, no more zombies'."

John Braine, *Room at the Top*

INTRODUCTION

It was never intended that we would do a second *Kitchen Sink Gothic* collection, but it was brought home to us when we were watching a production of *Rent* at the Oswaldtwistle Civic Theatre, directed by our daughter, Cassandra, just how bad the plight of the homeless is. The cast of this production went out with buckets to collect money during the intermission for a local homeless charity, Nightsafe, which concentrates on looking after some of the most vulnerable homeless, those under 21.

It was a little after this that I conceived the idea of doing a charity anthology of stories such as these. And *Kitchen Sink Gothic* seemed somehow a more than appropriate title for the book.

I must thank all of the writers who have submitted stories for it, both those who are in this book and those who, unfortunately, I had to reject, for being prepared to have their work published free of charge so that all of the royalties earned by it will go to charity.

I would also like to thank artist Allen Koszowski for providing our cover art, again, like the writers, free of charge.

Let me stress however, though none of the writers have or will be paid for these tales, don't think for one moment they are any the less excellent. I am proud of this collection, which I believe you will enjoy in many different ways. There are some bizarre stories here, and some that will wrench you emotionally, with sadness and anger and, yes, sometimes with horror too, while others will stimulate your imagination with the strange, dark worlds they evoke within our all too often humdrum world. The one thing I hope they never do is bore you.

So, please, with no more ado read on!

David A. Riley
Oswaldtwistle, October 2020

THE RING ON THE ROOF
James Harper

"What th –"

On the Henderson roof, Jake Buckley found something he had never seen before, a thing new and not like anything else in his experience. Using his finger to dig at the asphalt-coated shingle, he raised its flap to look at the tar paper covered plywood beneath when he saw it. It looked like nothing he had seen in his life: a raised round symbol, dark red and circular; it held the image of some kind of octopus – tentacles falling out of a bloated head – within a decorated ring as large as his expanded hand.

"What the fuck?" he said aloud.

The material felt like glass, but a kind he hadn't seen anywhere else; denser than normal glass, a deep rich burgundy colour came off it that changed in the light of the strong morning sun. Setting his footing on the steeply pitched roof, he pushed at it to see how secure it had been attached. It didn't budge. To Jake, who had done a little construction before he came to work for Salvatore at HomePro, it appeared that the ring had been firmly secured to the roof, not put there by accident. It's here for a reason, he thought.

The sunlight reflected a bright glow from the ring as Jake put his fingers to it, the surface warmed his fingers when, in an instance, he felt pain in his hand. His right hand cramped as he touched the material the ring was made of, not a serious cramp, but an unexpected one. It disappeared when he pulled his hand away. Shaking the hand, he stood upright on the roof, making his way across to locate more hail damage.

He'd have to work on the ring harder when he retrieved his tools from the truck. But now he wasn't about to climb down to fetch them just to figure this out, not when he had a roof to price.

"It can wait," he muttered.

And a decent roof it turned out to be too. The hailstorm that had come through the area during May a couple months back had rendered the roof as qualified for replacement; any insurance company, he felt, would approve this one. The pits from the hailstones were clearly evident on the shingles in areas larger than the six-foot minimum most home policies required. Jake felt confident the roof would go forward.

He circled the hail marks with the four-inch piece of white chalk he carried in the side pockets of his khaki cargo shorts, marking the places where the hail had pummelled the asphalt the worst. It was evident to him that the volume here fell within the guidelines insisted on by most insurance carriers. The owner downstairs had said that her carrier was Wayfarers. Jake was sure this roof would pass.

After taking shots of the qualifiers with his phone, he went back to the ring to shoot it as well. He changed his mind about going after the tools. This is a good roof, maybe twenty grand. At the end of the day, he thought, I really don't care about some weird ornament. Gimme the money, fuck the rest, he always said.

Clambering down the slope of the roof, he reached out with care to the ladder he had left at the gutter edge. With slow, practiced patience, he placed his foot on the rung, easing his weight onto it, then scaled down to the ground. He rang down the ladder, then hoisted it on his good shoulder to return it to the frame above the bed of his company pickup. A few minutes later, he sat in the dining room of the home speaking to the owner.

"I'll have to talk to my husband," the woman said. "He's going to want to hear about this."

Fuck me, Jake thought. Here it comes.

"Do you think you can come back later?"

Fuck me more, he thought but said, "Sure, no problem. When do you think he'll be home?"

"Oh, maybe 9:00."

Fuck. Another late night. Still, he thought, since it looked to be adding up to a twenty-grand roof, I got no problems swinging back.

"Okay sure, I can come back then. You want to sign the release?" He handed her the HomePro standard release that gave him permission to pursue the claim. "The sooner we put this in motion, the sooner your claim'll be approved."

She looked at the paper as if she had just eaten an ill-chosen pickle.

"Well, my husband should really be the one who signs anything. He's the owner. He bought the house fifteen years ago. We've only been married for less than a year."

Fuck me until Tuesday, Jake thought, this one's getting stinkier and stinkier. Still, twenty.

"Sure, no problem," he said through a forced smile. "I'll leave it here for you both to look at. Talk about it amongst yourselves. If you have any questions, here's my card." He handed her his business card.

Walking across the luxurious grass of their lawn back to his truck, Jake figured he'd work the best angles he could think of in anticipation of whatever objections the husband would bring. It's always the husbands who ruin the close, he thought, especially when they come into it after the wives.

13

Climbing behind the wheel, he started the engine then drove through the high-end suburban Mount Auburn neighbourhood called Tussman Estates. Each of the homes he passed boasted acre-and-a-half lawns on which stood homes that could only be afforded by the wealthiest of those who worked and lived in the Washington DC metropolitan area. The houses held forty-five rooms apiece, from the smallest kitchen alcove to the largest master bedroom.

Salvatore had identified the neighbourhood as the prime target for their effort to locate, confirm then sell new roofs to the homeowners who had been hit hardest by the May storm. That Salvatore and HomePro reaped the rewards of that calamity, so much the better. Jake went along for the ride since Salvatore paid a better than average percentage of the retail roof price. Jake didn't even mind the canvassing that came along with the roof jumping as long as his payday hit the numbers he expected.

His cell rang, singing Def Leppard's "Foolin'" into his ear. Salvatore.

"Hey, Salvatore."

"Jake." Salvatore never greeted; never said anything pleasant or kind, he merely barked whatever was on his short-spanned attention. "What happened with that house in Glen Meadow in Leighton?"

"I left a release with the couple. They wanted to think about it overnight."

"That was two days ago. Why haven't you been back there?"

Jesusfuckthisnoise, Jake thought. "Because I've had my hands full here, Salvatore." He ran through his internal check list. "I had an eval with Ameriwide at 8:00 this morning, a call back in Radford at 10:00 and I just got off a roof in Tussman Estates just now."

"How'd it go?"

Jake winced, knowing that when he finished the statement he was about to make, he'd be reprimanded. He took the slimmest of comforts in the recognition that, no matter what he said or did, the reprimand would come anyway. Nothing ever pleased Salvatore.

"I gotta go back tonight."

"What? Why?"

Jake closed his eyes and grinded his teeth. Then he said, "So he can sign the release."

"You mean you went up a roof when both owners weren't there?"

Jake drove aimlessly through the gridded streets of Tussman Estates, focused on his now-painful convo with Salvatore. He tried to remain mindful of the stop signs, but, if truth be told, he thought, he may have missed one or two in his ambling.

"Dude, she told me she was the owner before I even went up there," Jake said. "I made sure I asked her specifically," he lied. In fact, Jake never made that sort of determination, finding that getting up on the roof made the close easier even if not all the owning parties were present. This he did knowing it was against one of Salvatore's cardinal rules.

"'Always see a roof after seeing all the owners,'" Salvatore said with practiced rote.

"Right, right," Jake said. His experience had taught him that, at this point in the gruelling torture, it would be best if he just agreed with whatever Salvatore said. The excoriation only lasted as long as his attention span would allow and that, at its lengthiest, only went five minutes.

By rote, Jake repeated "yeah" and "right" while Salvatore droned on about the profit percentage and the necessity of maintaining a good average of roofs to climb up on. His own focus elsewhere, Jake looked for a spot of seclusion. Five minutes later, as if clocked on it, Salvatore hung up and Jake pulled into his hideaway.

Jake parked the truck on a wooded back road behind the sewage pumping station on the eastern perimeter of Tussman Estates. He fired up a pipe. As he smoked, he allowed the worries of a ruined close and the phone conversation with Salvatore to slide off his consciousness.

His day had stacked up pretty well, he thought. With the Ameriwide approval that morning and if the Hendersons come through – and he felt confident he could close it – he'd have a 50K day. That's good no matter what Salvatore would say.

So thinking, he slid the driver's seat back to relax while he smoked, closing his eyes as he lay back with an audible sigh. His cell chimed in a text, probably another roof appointment sent by Ashley. It'll wait, Jake thought, I need to do this right now.

After a half-hour, Jake made himself check the text. He stretched the fingers of his hand to relieve its numbness.

"Canvas rest tussman estates," the message from Salvatore read. Fuck, Jake thought, dreading the notion of walking from house to house in the ninety-degree heat. Still, after he finished the pipe, he went to it.

"You're one of those storm chasers, the guys out here trying to capitalize on the hailstorm. I read about you. You come out after a hailstorm to tell homeowners that they have hail damage then try to get them to replace their roofs."

The woman speaking to Jake wore the faded housecoat of a stay at home mom whose stay at home kids had long since gone on to college. Her nicotine-stained fingers twitched as she spoke to Jake, as if eager to end the conversation in order light up. Jake knew the feeling. He felt it himself, even if he didn't share the affection for the drug of choice.

He held his gloved hands up in a stop fashion. "Just a minute," he said, marshalling his patience by dredging up all the good will he could locate. "We're just out here trying to help folks that had their homes damaged in the storm."

"Where's your office?" she asked, reaching for the flyer as Jake handed it to her.

"Monroeville," he said by rote. "Just up the road, three townships away." He neglected to inform her that it was only a mail drop.

"Yeah, right," she said without conviction. She studied the slick flyer. Ashley had designed it to feature bright greens and blues with hints of browns and yellows, all the soothing buying trigger shades.

He said, "Look, some of the other companies that've been out here come from out of state: Pennsy and Ginny. So, I know about the – situation you're referring to." He stopped short of saying the word "scam." The unspoken rule of roof jumpers was to not call the others crooks.

She stopped looking at the flyer to face him. "Yeah, we're not interested." She closed the door as he opened his mouth again.

"Thank you so much, ma'am," he said to the closed door. He touched the brim of his cap.

The sun bore on his head as he crossed the yard into the next property. Canvassing in the July sun could qualify as enhanced interrogation tactics, he thought as he wiped his forehead.

"I've heard about you people," the next homeowner said to him as he stood on his stoop. He wore faded blue jeans under a wife beater with brown stains that Jake hoped were either coffee or chocolate. "You guys come out to neighbourhoods like ours and tell folks we got our roofs ruined in the hailstorm. Then you puts yer signs all over the yards in the Estates, so that that's all we see driving through the streets."

Jake opened his mouth to respond then thought better. The homeowner took a breath then continued.

"Then all our insurance rates goes up cause you gets the insurance companies to agree to replace the roofs. John Wilson over on Prospect Road told me all about it. That whole street's got PRs on the roofs doing replacements."

Almost groaning at the racism, Jake thought to point out that it wasn't the roof jumpers that made the insurance companies raise the rates; which they'd do regardless any time a hailstorm catastrophe is declared. But again he thought better. Fuck this guy, he thought.

"So we don't need nothing," the homeowner said. He stared at Jake, as if waiting for him to leave.

Jake recognized how fuck off could be reworded. "Have a nice day," he said, touching his brim.

"You guys been harassing all the neighbours I been talking to," the next homeowner said. He wore a red flannel shirt (in July?) over wrinkled khakis held up by an oversized belt the foot-long end of which dangled from his waist. "You been out here for weeks, banging on our doors, trying to sell us roofs we don't need. Then you'll take off fer parts unknown and we'll never hear from you again."

As if you'd want to, Jake thought. Instead he said, "Sir, we've been a part of the community for over ten years. You can check out our web page with comments from our satisfied customers. You can also check us out on Angie's List."

"Our roof is fine," the owner said, closing the door as Jake stood there.

Minutes later, he reached out to ring the doorbell of the next house, a vinyl-sided three door with a chimney and wraparound porch. While rare, it wasn't as unique as the Henderson house.

At that moment, Jake stopped, his thinking now clearer. That's what had been lurking in the back of his mind. Structurally, the Henderson house had significant differences from the other houses in Tussman Estates. He had noticed the differences, but it wasn't until now, just this moment, that he put those differences together.

The Henderson house, and some others he had passed while tooling through the development, were built in the early Twentieth Century, the architecture and framing, along with their size and building materials, all spoke to the care and thought given to homes constructed as homes, not houses built to make money like the one where he stood now. Jake had remembered seeing at least two others in the area as he had worked the neighbourhood.

Adjusting his sunglasses, he walked off the porch. Abandoning the canvassing altogether, he decided he would find the other old houses.

An hour later, he stopped the truck by the curb on Park Ridge Lane to assess the information he'd gathered. There looked to be about ten to a dozen old early homes, each built with that same quality and craftsmanship not seen in any recent construction. Jake considered these anchor homes, the first houses built in the community that still stood after the developer who erected Tussman Estates bought the rest of the land ten to fifteen years ago.

Now that Jake had looked for it, it seemed real easy to find: the well-crafted homes appeared once on each of the ten or eleven streets in the development, usually on a corner or an end. In most cases, they stood at the beginning of an intersection or new street, as if a welcome or guardian to the homes on that block.

Like the one where Jake parked in front of now. Its classic good looks clearly evident now that he had looked for it.

It had a steep, hand-guided gable out front that pitched the roof in a way that gave it a handsome appearance at first glance. The porch it featured was long and wide while the doors had at least two inches on their contemporaries. In each case as here, an arched atrium window stood above the entranceway to allow the morning sun. Jake knew that this meant the back of the house had been designed to foster the cool of the evening, a characteristic lost on modern home designers whose interest in profit far outweighed any thought toward the subtleties of comfort. That architecture class at Garfield County Community College paid off anyway, he thought, a passing grade unnecessary.

There were more features to it that Jake noticed but rather than run through them all, he figured he'd focus on pitching and securing the roof work on all of these guys, since they would bring in the most money the quickest. He got out of the truck to knock on the door.

"No thanks," the owner, a man in his late forties, said. "I checked it myself. We got no damage." He closed the door before Jake could counter with his expertise.

Jake pulled the notebook with the anchor home addresses from his back pocket. Opening to the page that carried this address 11625 Meadowgreen Drive, he wrote a checkmark beside it. He drove to the next one, 37112 Whitetail Court on the next block over.

There, the owner wasn't home. He stood at the front

door, leaving a doorknob hanger. Then he stepped backward into the front yard to scan the roof from that position. It looked old, maybe 30 years, maybe older, with many streaks of mildew darkening the grey colour of the shingles. Age, however, didn't mean damage. So, he knew, he'd have to come back to get permission to get up there.

At the next house, he struck gold. Not only were both owners present, they both were eager to get the roof inspected.

"I'll just get my ladder to jump up there and have a look," he said after thanking them.

"Yeah, we've been hearing about how the hailstorm might drive down property values," the husband, Martin Statlin, said.

"We were a little concerned about that," the wife, Stephanie, put in. "We just caught such a big break in finding this home in the first place."

"Really?" Jake said without any real interest. His thoughts now led to the roof climbing he was about to engage in.

The wife said, "Yeah, we literally got it for a song."

"Yeah," Statlin said. "If it weren't for a relative in the real estate market who tipped us early to the house's availability, we wouldn't have caught such a break on the price."

Whatever, Jake thought. He walked to the truck to get the ladder. Pulling the aluminium ladder off the frame that it had been secured to, it clanged loudly as he slid it off. Setting it to the side of the pickup, he slipped into the truck cab to put on his Cougars and roofing gloves, both with Velcro-like adhesive that facilitated clinging to roofs.

Minutes later he walked the roof. He saw hail

damage for sure, the pock marks left by the icy precipitation had rendered the shingles scarred in the wake of the storm. The hardest hit section, like all the others in Tussman Estates, was the eastern portion of the roof, since it bore the brunt of the storm's leading edge.

After circling the dents with his chalk, Jake shot pictures with his cell. These he'd show to the Statlins to give them an idea of the extent of the damage which, Jake felt confident, their insurance company would approve for replacement.

Then he moved toward the top ridge of the house. At a point where the apex pointed to the north, he poked his hand around the area, touching the shingles to find a ring. Then he did; his hand felt the hard glass of the ring symbol beneath one of the shingles. He raised it from the tarpaper beneath.

Again he saw a round glass ring, this time its colour a rich blue sapphire that gleamed in the mid-day glare. Different colours make this little mystery even more interesting, he thought. He stooped closer to get a better look. Iridescent, it shined as he examined it. Within the circle he found another sea creature, this time he thought it a squid, its mouth hidden by tentacles that extended out of its head. Weird, Jake thought. He shot it about a dozen times.

Back with the owners in the living room, he sat on their large sofa. "You definitely have damage." He showed them the shots. "These are classic marks that we've been finding on roofs all over the area."

"Wow," the wife said.

"How much is up there? I mean, how many of the shingles will you have to replace?"

Jake smiled. "Oh, you're going to get a whole new roof."

"Really?"

"Yeah, in cases like this, after the insurance company confirms the storm damage then approves a new roof. You won't pay a penny."

"But won't our rates go up?"

Jake paused before responding. He did this for emphasis.

"Mr. Statlin, the truth is your rates are going to go up anyway. This whole side of the county got hit by that hailstorm on May 22nd. The weather service called it a catastrophe. There isn't an insurance company in the state that's not going to raise the rates of everyone in the area. You might as well take advantage of it."

He paused again, this time to let that sink in. Then he presented the release form. "Now, if you just sign here, we can get started." He handed them the paper. "The sooner we get on this, the sooner you get your new roof."

"Okay, great," Statlin said as he took the release. He placed it on the coffee table to sign it. Jake restrained the urge to stare at this, knowing the perceived greed might squelch the deal. Ms. Statlin also signed. His heart speeding up a click or two with the thrill of the close, Jake folded the release then made it disappear into one of the pockets of his cargos.

"Thank you so much," he said.

"How much do you think we'll get?"

Jake smiled inwardly. It never fails, he thought.

"The insurance companies have a software they use to calculate all the factors going into the replacement of a roof. They factor in size, location, storm damage, age of the house – that sort of – um –" Jake lost the word he wanted.

"Criteria?"

"Right, criteria," he said. "So they take all these criterias into consideration when they figure out how much to pay for the replacement roof."

"Oh, so we have to wait for the insurance company to come out?" Ms. Statlin asked.

"Well, the insurance company's going to be coming out anyway when you file your claim. Give them a call, let them know that HomePro's been out to look at your roof and they'll send out an agent to make their own assessment."

"Do you think we'll get approved?" Mr. Statlin asked. Jake knew he had talked to one of his neighbours when he asked this question. Someone else in the neighbourhood had sweated out the approval process then told Statlin about it.

"Depends. Who did you say your insurance company is?"

"FarmState."

"Right, FarmState. Yeah, the FarmState guy in this area is Bill Reynolds. I have a pretty good working relationship with Bill. I think we can work together to get you approved."

"Great," Mr. Statlin said.

"Oh, good," she said.

Time to GTFO, Jake thought. I need a pipe. He stood to head for the front door.

"So, I'm just going to head out. If you have any questions, here's my card; that's my cell number right there. Give me a call if you have any concerns or questions about the process. I'll get the rest of the paperwork started."

On cue, the Statlins showed him the biggest smiles he had seen in the conversation. Happens every time, he thought.

Out at his truck, he replaced the ladder on top of the frame over his pickup bed, the hard-forged aluminium clangs echoed against the houses. Climbing back into the cab, he checked his cell: two texts and five calls from Salvatore. Fuck, he thought; it's one of *those* days.

The first text read: Henderson at Village Oaks called. U fuckd up they ddnt want you there

The second read: Call me

Jake didn't bother listening to the voice mails. He already knew their content and tone would just piss him off. Salvatore's practice of leaving barking orders and condescending criticism – even in the face of good work – never failed to put Jake in a bad mood.

He didn't deserve a bad mood right now; he had just signed a roof. He considered calling to shove that into Salvatore's face. He decided to text instead.

"5371 Rising Ridge Road signed. Looks 35K."

"Nice," came the reply from Salvatore. Way to compliment a guy, Salv, Jake thought as he started the truck engine. That would keep him off his ass for at least the rest of the afternoon. He drove back to the outskirts of the development.

Here in the wooded recesses of the county where the edges of the exurb growth spurt met the forest realms of deer, fox and crow, Jake stopped the truck then reached for his pipe. Firing it up, within his thoughts, he sighed as he inhaled. Fuck them all, he thought as he drifted.

The woods he had parked in lulled him into that revelry that allowed him to forget, at least for the moment, the bashings from Salvatore and the inhumanities perpetrated by the customers he canvassed. He watched into the woods as the birds flitted from the branches and the sun beamed through the leaves. Part of him wished that he could just blow off the day to sit here looking at all this serenity. But, he knew, he wouldn't make 100K this year if he spent his days doing that.

Thirty minutes later, he went back to it. Looking at the list he had created, he chose to head over to 11128 Rambling Sunset Circle, a corner prop standing high at the top of the rise that dominated the whole Tussman development.

Driving there, he stopped so suddenly, the tires of the truck screeched, sending an echo through the Estates. At the corner of the first street into Tussman stood a church, a larger than normal structure erected in the same style and design as the anchor homes. To Jake's eye, the same architect had designed the anchors.

Black and gloomy, it loomed behind the trees like a monolith raised by Polynesians, its sharp roof edges jutting into the sky at angles Jake hadn't seen before. Shaking off a shudder, he looked to the sign for the denomination. Ichthys, Church of the Holy Fisher, the sign read. Wonder if the same guy built it along with the anchors, he thought.

At the Rambling Sunset address, he was met at the door of the house by a young woman who fell into that marginal age range that always confused him. Wearing a short skirt and a halter that spoke of her plan to sun outside on the pool deck in her backyard, the woman appeared to be in her mid-twenties, making her either the daughter of a middle-aged couple who would be the owners or the young wife who was herself the owner.

Jake decided that to determine this may prevent him from getting on the roof. His personal goal always was to get on the roof. Worry about all the rest of it later, he always said, because, once you're on the roof; once you've established the need for a replacement, you can deal with all the other shit that comes down afterward, even Salvatore's bad mood.

"Good afternoon," he said. "I'm Jake Buckley with HomePro. We're in the neighbourhood helping out your neighbours over on Rising Ridge Road –" He pointed vaguely over his shoulder. "They got clobbered with the hailstorm that came through here in May. We were able to work with their insurance company to get them a new roof. So, we thought that, since we're in the area, we'd stop by to make sure that you didn't get hit with the same kind of damage they did."

The standard spiel/pitch designed to create desire and need through implied threat and fear of loss. He had honed it over time for maximum impact.

The woman smiled. "Well, I guess you'd better have a look then, shouldn't you?"

He returned her smile – she's cute, he thought – as he walked back to his truck to retrieve his ladder. After putting on his Cougars and gloves, he hoisted the ladder on his shoulder, then trudged back to the house. This one looked a lot like the other anchor houses with a wraparound and wide door frames. The angles of the roof were steep too, like the last house he climbed up on. He slammed the ladder against the gutter.

He pulled on the pulley rope, the tether that drew the ladder to its longest length in a one-man operation. Then he scrambled to the roof edge making sure to secure the ladder to the gutter with his bungee ties.

Up on the roof, he saw the damage right away. Yeah, this is a keeper, he thought as he chalked the pock marks. The shingles looked like they hadn't been replaced in over thirty years, much longer than the normal lifespan of a modern roof.

After assuring that the roof needed replacement, he scuttled up to the highest point on the pitch. Then, like the others, he found the glass ring, this time a deep dark green. It glistened in the sun as he uncovered it from beneath the shingle. He thought that the image looked somehow different too, like it seemed to be a different kind of octopus or a cuttlefish, another type of creature altogether. He cracked the knuckles of one hand to bring back sensation.

Jake shrugged. Fuck it, he thought. As long as these older anchor homes keep giving him roofs he can close – homeowners he can sell to – he didn't care what these rings were really. In the bigger picture, they were only a curiosity anyway. He scampered down the roof.

He rang the doorbell. She came to the door wearing the same smile she offered him earlier. Jake liked the friendly ones. Since most of the people he spoke to seemed to be angry or grumpy or mean or hostile, whenever he was approached with friendliness, he felt good.

She allowed him in. As he passed her on the threshold, he caught the scent of her long blonde hair; it carried the freshness of lavender soap. Beneath that, her cologne made Jake weak, the smell buckling his knees. He wanted to stand there on the spot to drink her in, his eyes closed to the feast of her presence and her smell.

"What did you say your name was?"

"Jake. Jake Buckley. You can call me Jake." He winced knowing the stupidity of the unnecessary last sentence.

"Well, Jake, why don't you come into the kitchen?" She motioned in the direction.

At the kitchen, he stopped to take it in. A huge cantilever ceiling rose to large oak crossbeams that supported the walls. An enormous gas stove stood on one side while a cooking island larger than any he had ever seen held sway in the centre of the floor. If this was an indication of what the rest of the house looked like, he thought, he was impressed.

"Nice kitchen," he said.

"Thanks." She came around from behind him, brushing his arm as she stepped past. She turned to face him, reaching for his crotch as she leaned toward his neck. Gently, she bit his ear.

One of Jake's other rules – one of the hard and fast ones – was never turn down a serious offer. He spent the next hour upstairs in the master bedroom in her company.

Afterward, as he buckled the belt to his khakis, he spotted a book on the dresser. The cover read "Ichthys."

"What's this?"

She bounced on the bed they had run to earlier. "Oh, that's just our scripture. We believe in the Holy Fisher who teaches submission and release. Because we are their thousand young, the gods will come for us one day." She tucked her legs under her butt, leaning forward, palms on her knees. She smiled at him.

That's when he remembered. "You know, we never did get around to talking about your roof."

"Oh yeah. You're going to have to talk to my mom and dad about that. They're the owners of the house."

Jake leaned his head back on his shoulders to stare at the ceiling. Fuck, he thought.

Later, climbing back into the cab of his truck, he tempered the disappointment he had felt with the pleasure he had enjoyed. He counselled himself that this kind of thing didn't happen every day. Or ever, really.

He drove himself to the nearest Five Guys for a burger and fries. Squeezing down the double cheese with onions and green peppers within four minutes, he picked at the fries while he figured out what to do next. Unless a text from Ashley came through directing him to another location, he didn't have anything on his agenda until he had to go back to the Henderson house on Village Oaks at 9:00.

Wait. Didn't Salvatore text him about that? He checked his cell.

"Henderson at Village Oaks called. U fuckd up they ddnt want you there" Fuck.

He dialled Salvatore. He picked up after one ring.

"Jake."

"What did the Hendersons say at Village Oaks?"

"Village Oaks? Where's that?" Already Salvatore's notorious short-attention span had lost the information.

"Tussman Estates."

"Oh yeah. Yeah, they called. They said that they didn't even want you up their roof."

"No, that's not right. The wife was right there. She gave me permission."

"She was there?"

"Yes, Salvatore. That's what I just said. She was there. She gave me permission. She wanted me to take a look at her roof." He kept the sentences short and to the point. He only had four more minutes to go in this conversation.

"Well, the husband called all pissed off that you went up there."

"Can't help that. The wife said it was okay."

"You're sure?"

"Positive." He said nothing more. Sometimes Salvatore needed to be closed too.

"So the wife gave you permission."

"That's what I just said."

"All right. Fine."

Jake allowed himself a smile.

"Go back and close the husband."

Jake wanted to say, "That was my plan all along you retard!" Instead he said, "Will do."

He clicked off to begin his hunt to find another smoke spot. While he liked the ones he had gone to before, he had learned that high-end neighbourhoods pay attention to frequent visits by repeat visitors, particularly those that drove pickup trucks emblazoned with full-body advertising like his HomePro Ford was. So, he searched for then located a side road about a mile from Tussman Estates.

The summer sun dipped below the woods to the west, casting shadows on the truck in the back road. Jake lit his pipe to inhale deeply, closing his eyes as he held the smoke in his lungs. He exhaled, allowing another smile as his brain received the rush he had been eagerly wanting. Fuck them all, he thought as he eased the driver seat back, I'm going to go back to the Henderson house when I'm finished here then I'm done for the day.

He checked the weather report for the next day on his cell. Rain. Perfect. Roofers, both those who inspect and those who install, do not work in the rain for safety reasons. Roofs are difficult to maintain a balance on in the best of circumstances even with wearing Cougars and special gloves; rain makes it impossible. So, he'd spend the next day catching up with insurance paperwork, filing claims with the various agencies and registering with the local adjusters. No canvassing, no calling on homes, he'd spend the day in his underwear watching porn.

When it was 8:30, he started the truck then drove back to the Henderson home. He expected an unhappy husband, so he prepared to kill him with kindness: to project as happy and as pleasant a demeanour as possible, even in the face of anger or belligerence.

Mr. Henderson answered the door even before Jake had finishing ringing the doorbell, not a good sign, he thought. Nonetheless, he wore his widest, biggest smile.

"Mr. Henderson? Good evening." He fingered the brim of his cap.

"Oh, you," Henderson said as he stood in the doorframe. He wore a striped business shirt over suit slacks that cost as much as Jake made in a day during a good week. "Listen, your coming here this afternoon was a mistake. You shouldn't have been here and you had no business going up on my roof."

Jake widened his smile until his cheeks hurt. "Well, I'm terribly sorry about the misunderstanding, Mr. Henderson –"

"Misunderstanding? There's no misunderstanding. You were up on my roof without my permission. You're lucky I don't have you arrested right now for trespassing."

Holy fuck, Jake thought. He had heard hard lines before but not this extreme and never this early in the process. He adopted a defensive posture, holding his hands up in front of him in a mock surrender.

"Again, Mr. Henderson, I'm really sorry for the misunderstanding."

Still managing to maintain his best cordial manner in a kind of fuck-you underpinning, in his calmest tone, Jake said, "Sir, if you want to discuss it, we can talk about as you wish. You know, like civilized people in a reasonable way." Jake had found these words usually did well in calming down irate potential customers. "As I said, I'm sorry." He smiled.

Henderson's shoulders slumped slightly. He looked down at Jake's feet. "Well, I guess we can do that." He turned to allow him in the house.

"Thank you, sir," Jake said as he crossed the threshold. Henderson motioned for the living room; Jake complied.

"Have a seat," Henderson said.

Jake sat on the softest, most comfortable couch he had ever sat on; his sun-drenched back thanked him for the relaxing sensation. He still wore his best smile. He might salvage this roof sale yet.

"Let me ask you just real quick," Henderson said, "did you find or see anything unusual while you were up on our roof?"

"As a matter of fact, I did." He remembered the ring.

Henderson gave Jake a grave look. "Well, that changes everything. There's nothing I can do for you."

He leaned toward Jake and said, "Now."

Pain shot through Jake, making him bolt to his feet. A shock of distress flowed throughout his body as he stood.

Standing in the living room, Jake looked at his hands. Something emerged from beneath his fingernails, tiny pricks of pain erupted under his skin as he pulled his fingers closer to his eyes to get a better look. Out of the ends of his fingers, from under the nails, tiny, almost microscopic worms burst through his skin, emerging from holes as they created hundreds of bleeding ruptures.

So tiny he had to hold his hand up to his face to see them clearly, he gasped as he looked. The heads of the worms appeared bulbous with tentacles coming out of the mouths. They squirmed across his skin in the hundreds then thousands, covering his body. They looked like octopus heads on tiny maggots.

In a matter of seconds, his fingertips became ragged tatters of blood and worms, their infinitesimal bodies crawling over his hands as they spread across his skin. He tried to shake them off, throwing his hand at the floor in a quick motion to cast them off. But with tenacity, they held onto him, spreading all across his arm and up his shoulder. In mere moments, they had attacked his face, beginning to cover his head.

Then Jake felt them chew.

The tiny worms, if that's what they were, began to eat Jake, to gnaw on his skin, to consume his head, to gobble his flesh. A million stabbing pains covered Jake in agony as he screamed out, his body a mass of hurting, agonizing pieces of torture. They stripped off his skin in ribbons, working together in a manic unison that had them pull a layer of his skin from the muscle beneath, consume it greedily, then repeat the process.

He doubled over, clutching his belly as if some unseen blow had been struck there. Then, from within his abdominal cavity, another surge of worms emerged, breaking his skin to explode over his body. These were larger, the size of pinheads, spreading over his body and his clothes to cover him as they, too, began to eat.

They stripped the flesh from the outer part of his skin, eating his epidermis in a swollen mass of all-consuming, all-controlling pain. As Jake watched on in helpless horror, the tiny beings squiggled and crawled on his hands, his face, his legs and his skin. The fingers now all eaten, Jake saw mere bones left, the meat of his flesh gone.

Falling to his knees, Jake felt them squish, crushed beneath his weight. But their numbers were too great, millions of them covered him, eating, chewing, biting in countless painful mouthfuls, tearing him to pieces in a less time than it took for him to breath a hundred breathes.

Jake, desperate, agonized, tried to think of a something, anything, that would save him from this pain, something that would stop this torture. The pain prevented that, the overwhelming agony causing him to think of only it, it was all he could know, all that he could realize in this moment.

He felt more stream from his mouth, these larger than the others, pouring out of his mouth in a continuous run. He reached to his head, holding his skull against the pain. As he did so, he realized that they had eaten his hair; it was all gone from his scalp. They had begun to eat that too.

Helpless, Jake held his hands before his face, the skin on his fingers also gone now, the bone leering through in blood-covered white. He screamed and screamed.

Standing over Jake's body, Henderson did not answer back.

THE CHRISTMAS TREE
Eric Nash

December 26th 20 —

Lucy gurgled. Crying didn't achieve what it was supposed to anymore. She heard the key in the back door – she'd heard the doorbell ring as well and knew it would stop when it grew tired of being ignored. The face of the resonating voice did not come to her. The calling out of names she recognised was a worry. He shouted; she cried, startled in that sudden freeze kind-of-way by a bombardment of footfalls on the stairs.

"Jean! Sam!"

"Yes, ambulance, please.

"Taylor!

"Lucy? Lucy."

When Lucy's eyes opened he stood over her. Dropped the slim, black thing into which he'd spoken and lifted her up in his arms. The beat of his heart was disturbing, yet his smell calmed her cries to short, sudden gasps as salty splashes fell on her wet face.

*

The last sighting of a ghost in the grounds of St Bartholomew's church on Midwinter Hill happened on Christmas Day that year, when Darrell Jenkins of no fixed abode saw *a dedicated husband and beloved dad* hold the hand of a *devoted wife and much-missed mum*. At their feet a three-foot-tall Norwegian Spruce flourished upright in its red plastic bucket. A rat's tail of tinsel and four lengths of cotton thread hung from the vibrant evergreen.

"We've must've missed Christmas," the wife said, dressed in her Sunday best.

"Council takes Christmas trees if you leave 'em out, Norah. Bloody nerve of some people just dumping the thing here."

The wife rested her head on her husband's shoulder. "Well, it seems to like it here, Ken. I do love Christmas."

The couple were so full of life that Darrell had not understood he'd been looking upon the dead.

*

The previous day Jean and her eldest, Sam, became as listless as Taylor. There was little point going to the doctor, they didn't do hand-outs anymore when kids got sick. There isn't much I can do, Mrs Smith, the GP had said in the past, my advice is to give them lots of rest and plenty of fluids. The more sick as children, the healthier as adults.

Lucy had been crying for some time, but the good thing about disposable nappies when compared to the Terry equivalent which Sam had worn, was they were very absorbent.

Not long after the knife incident, Jean really could not see the use of getting out of bed; life was better under the duvet even if it did smell stale. She didn't think much after that.

*

The headline on the front cover of the newspaper tumbling between the headstones on the 23rd, announced, 'The Dead Celebrate Christmas!' The accompanying photo featured a delightful Christmas tree in St Bart's churchyard, though its decorations appeared misshapen and blackened. The warden picked it up and shoved it in his bin liner with the rest of the litter. On his way toward the wooden archway at the end of the path and his car beyond, he witnessed the revenant of a soldier – *a beloved son* – salute the church wall. The buttons on the ghost's forage cap and the metal on his gaiters glinted in the low sun. If it were not for these details, and the way the man sometimes faded, the warden could have mistaken the soldier for a mourner.

At the same time Sam cut himself to see how deep pain goes with the penknife his dad gave him the year before.

*

Jean had presents to wrap. She would do that tomorrow. Although, if she told the children she had cancelled Christmas until they were all feeling better, they could concentrate on recuperating, knowing that they would have a fabulous time in a few days. Jean was sure that Sam and Taylor wouldn't be too disappointed.

*

The promise of bubble-gum ice cream didn't tempt Taylor downstairs because his head only throbbed when upright.

While he drifted in and out of sleep, Mrs Howell noticed that someone had left a Christmas tree on one of the graves. Perky little thing, decorations had seen better days, though. It was a nice thought. Between visiting her deceased husband and her interred lover, she spied a ghostly pair of twins hop upon the sepulchre of a *much-loved and greatly missed* fellow. There they fought a thumb war. The girl on the right squeezed the sister's hand so tightly that the sibling bit her own lip.

Greeting cards portraying Father Christmas and winter scenes lay unopened on the carpet in the Smith's hallway, their red, white and green envelopes added festive colour to the grubby, oatmeal fabric. Some had postmarks, others not.

*

With Lucy and without a wage there hadn't been many Amazon deliveries in the run-up to the season. Less to wrap - a small blessing. Jean felt really quite exhausted the last day or so. The newspaper and the glitter still had to be cleared before she could think about using the table. At least, the tree was done. Jean attributed the reason for her lethargy to the bug going around – another mild winter – it also explained why, on the few occasions the boys emerged from their rooms, they appeared pasty.

*

The first sighting of a ghost on Midwinter Hill in one hundred and fifty-nine years happened when Jean stumbled over the words in the story book like she was traipsing through mud. A *loving mother and beloved wife* rose from her modest plot on the north side of the church. She stood there with a pallid countenance, so said a dog-walker on his way home from the Midford Arms.

*

Jean attributed the lapses in memory to her fuzzy head. Kids were forgetful as a rule, especially teenagers.

An arrangement with a friend had slipped her mind and so she had to rush to be no more than half hour late. Her friend presented a small gift to Jean, putting her in the embarrassing situation of not having one in exchange, nor had she given the slightest thought to buying a present. The visit was short-lived. Sam and Taylor came scuffing back early from the park with her friend's two, all four were arguing. Jean realised that squabbling had become the commonest denominator.

After a take-away dinner, Sam loped off to shoot the undead on his PS4, before glazing over watching YouTube in bed. She often wondered why she let him watch it; people uploaded the strangest, most pointless things.

Taylor tried to build a racing car with his Lego. The attempt slid into failure, the instructions swept aside, the car turned into a tank-thing that was inevitably hit by a long-range fist. The bricks dug into the ball of his hand, but he didn't cry. Nor when Jean shouted at him, but he stared at her, stunned.

Jean attempted to read a bedtime story to Lucy. She loved to admire the textured, plump illustrations in *Dogger* by Shirley Hughes, because they reminded her of childhood's joyful simplicity, but that day they only framed disappointments and lies.

*

In the short time since it had been placed on fertile soil, the Spruce appeared straighter and had swelled, its needles boasted an increase in glossiness and its perfume became a heady mixture of ripe fruit. Upon its lush branches, the baubles seemed… dull.

41

The Smiths travelled back through a grotto filled with the town's houses and gardens decked with festive illuminations. The children's father used to haul them on an annual neighbourhood tour instead of putting his hand in his pocket to buy their own lights. Nonetheless, the sight normally brought warmth and magic to the gloom of a winter's dusk and had the whole family tingling with expectation. Returning from Midwinter Hill, however, the festive displays were as drab as wet shingle on a beach and the view through the windscreen, a murky puddle that reminded her of childhood holidays gazing out of misted caravan windows streaming with rain.

Jean stemmed the outburst of sibling bickering by hot, milky chocolate and movies under the duvet. The overall mood remained low and led to an early teeth-and-bed for the boys and a bath for Jean after Lucy finally settled.

Afterward, Jean regarded the glitter and glue and newspaper all over the kitchen table knowing it was unlike her to leave it a mess. She hoped her parents would like the tree. Some may think it weird to do it, but her mum had so loved Christmas, and Jean loved her very much. She turned off the lights.

*

Loaded with two kids, a baby, supplies, a bootful of tools, coats and wellies, and a Christmas tree, the little Ford almost died climbing up the hill to the churchyard.

"Ooh, we might have to walk." Jean laughed.

"I'll die if I have to walk up this hill."

"Don't be silly, Taylor. Your Nanna used to march up here every Sunday."

"Nanna's dead."

Sam replied, "Well, it wasn't the walking that killed her, Taylor."

"Nah,nah,nah,nah."

"Taylor!"

Black-as-pen-and-ink silhouettes of trees swayed against the panorama of slush-coloured cloud, their branches like bare and crooked snowman arms waving in greeting. Gravel crunched under tyres, and the perfume of decay emanating from the damp woods filled the family's reddening nostrils when departing the cocoon of the car. Jean carried the tree through the archway; Sam pushed Lucy; Taylor dragged the baubles until Jean told him to lift the bag up before he broke them. Their expressions told her they wished they had hats and gloves. Maybe next time they would listen.

Jean plucked brittle leaves from her parents' grave. Kenneth and Norah had paid a princely sum for their simple double kerb memorial with green glass chipping infill on the north aspect, and her dad had waited fifteen years for his wife to join him in their final investment. There was still time to find someone whom Jean would want to be beside for eternity.

"I'm freezing," said Taylor.

"Do your coat up, Taylor, like I asked you, and give me a hand with the tree."

"If I ran around, I'd warm up."

"Afterwards, please."

Taylor dropped the carrier bag and helped his mum place the Norwegian Spruce at his grandparents' feet.

"Now they can see it, Tay. That'll put a smile on their faces, won't it?"

The Spruce fell over.

"It's fallen over, Mum."

Taylor handed out the baubles to Jean and Sam after they'd collected a few stones to ramp up against the bucket. Jean and Sam sang *Silver Bells*, her Mum's favourite Christmas carol. Taylor blew raspberries, though they were in tune, which wasn't to be said for Lucy's grumbles. After that, Taylor ran off.

Sam stayed with his mum by the graveside. He knew where his younger brother was headed, and not so long ago he would have joined him there, but maybe some memories were best left to fade away.

"You okay, Sam?"

"Yep. You?"

"I am. It looks grand, doesn't it?" she said, returning a tissue to her coat pocket. It looked out of place. It looked like Christmas trees do in January, but Sam didn't say that. His dad would have. From inside one of the other baubles, her photograph smiled at them both.

"Very grand," he replied, "you did good, Mum."

"*We* did good." Jean wrapped the branches in tinsel, securing it with a peg. "Go find your brother and let's go home."

Jean could not help but give her parents a last glance when she reached the car, similar to the ritual of looking in the rear view when leaving their house every Sunday afternoon, to see them smiling, waving goodbye.

If Jean believed her eyes, she'd admit to seeing the spruce rotate and sink firmly into the plot. Had Norah Smith, renowned for liking things 'just right', been irritated by the lackadaisical manner in which the tree had been potted, and sought to fix it? Jean hoped so.

*

It was the first day of the school holidays and the family had planned to decorate the tree. While Lucy slept, Jean found the *Now That's What I Call Christmas* CD, and adjusted the volume. Sam and Taylor were not as considerate when choosing photos of them all to put into four clear plastic baubles, and even less when they hauled out the art chest. Jean had words, but she knew they all struggled to keep quiet when crafting, and they were excited to be doing something for their Nanna and Grandpa. Still, babies were sound sleepers, especially when their parents were awake.

Taylor grabbed the felt tips and drew holly and snowmen and a big fat bearded fellow on his plastic bauble. It was an... enthusiastic effort. Nearly the entire contents of the PVA glue pot landed on the bauble so he could roll it in red, green, and the leftover Hallowe'en glitter.

Jean admired his 'accidental' creations. "Leave a space so Nanna and Grandad can see your photo," she said.

Her attempt was a sparkling, snowy window. Only a small circle, the size of her mother's cameo ring that she wore on her little finger, wasn't dusted with glitter and through this Jean's image regarded her.

It was a pretty decoration, Sam told her, but not edible like his. He had remained traditional, ignored the gaudy glitter, and replicated a Christmas pudding similar to those Nanna used to make. His fingers were stained by ink that would take several washes to come out.

Jean wasn't surprised when the boys decided they didn't want to decorate Lucy's. Her baby daughter's deserved to be elegant. She also admitted to being a big kid and wanted to have another bauble to personalise.

Lucy woke up when Jean hung the decorations above the radiator.

*

The three-foot-tall Norwegian Spruce leaned so far over its red plastic bucket that Sam propped it against the sofa to keep the tree upright.

"You sure they'll like it if it's wonky?" he asked. "Sorry."

His dad used to say stuff like that. He knew that Jean had wanted to decorate Nanna and Grandad's grave for some time, or he should have done; she'd reminded Sam's dad for months that the dead needed to know they were still thought of. His dad had replied that the deceased didn't need to know nowt 'cos they were dead. It didn't matter what that man said anymore because he'd left them all just after Sam's twelfth birthday. You'll still see me, he'd promised the kids, and just maybe it wasn't for Sam that she still left the spare back door key under the flowerpot. Sam wanted to believe in his dad, like Taylor still did, but Sam would be thirteen in a month's time.

"Of course, they'll like it, Sam."

"Why haven't *we* got a real Christmas tree?" Taylor asked as he watched the Spruce slide to the carpet again.

"Our luxury, eight foot, pre-lit, snowy, artificial one not good enough?"

"We've had it ages. I want a real one, Sam*wise*."

"No, you don't. They fall over."

"Yes, I—"

"They're special, aren't they Taylor?" Jean said. "Like Nanna and Grandad are special to us. It's important to show this to them. Remind them, that they're still remembered."

VLOG'S LEGS
Shaun Avery

"And that, my friends, is how you make an awesome meal using somebody's face."

Cody, grinning behind the camera, used his free hand to give me a thumbs-up.

And within seconds he'd uploaded the video, put it out there into the world. And I should have been excited, looking forward to all the new likes and comments we would get. Just like all the other times we'd done this.

But I guess that was the problem.

A dozen videos in and it still seemed like we were going nowhere.

But this time, though I did not yet know it . . .

This time would be different.

We'd met at a course we'd both been sent to by the Job Place – a course for both the long-term unemployed and the *professionally* unemployed... you know the type, those guys and girls who had built their lives around not having a job, who dropped out of school without sitting any exams and wore their ignorance like some bizarre badge of honour. Which instantly irritated the both of us, just one look between me and Cody enough to show that we did not belong there with these types.

So, I took a seat next to him, politely declining the one offered to me by the guy with "fuck" and "twat" tattooed – and misspelled – on his knuckles.

"Hey," Cody said, smiling at me. "They make you come too?"

"Yeah." I smiled back. "Name's James."

"Pleased to meet you, James. I'm Cody." We shook, and then he asked, "Ever get Jimmy?"

"Not for a while," I said. Not since school, in fact. Only one teacher had ever called me that, and I'd hated the guy. The lesson he taught, too. My hands just weren't built for Design Technology. Which was probably one of the reasons I had gone into office work rather than manual labour, heading straight into employment when I was sixteen, rising from office junior to team leader... only to be forced into unemployment when the company went belly-up. And to say that the world of job-hunting was proving to be a culture shock would be something of an under-statement.

He went to say something more. But then the course leader – a sour-faced old battle-axe who looked as unhappy as the rest of us about being there – entered the room.

Fast-forward past eight hours of mind-numbing, soul-killing tedium and Cody and I both breathed deeply of the outside air when we got out of there. Politely declining the tattooed man again, this time when he offered us drugs or knock-off tracksuit bottoms or both, we decided instead to go for a drink.

"Is that allowed when you're on benefits?" I asked.

"Not if you believe TV," he replied, grinning.

I was starting to like the guy already.

That was when we began hanging out, sharing the misery of our fruitless job search together. I was between girlfriends – quite a long gap between them, in fact – so I had no one to question how much time we were spending together, and Cody *did* have a girlfriend, a girl called Cecelia, but he spent his nights with her when she finished work, leaving his days free for me.

Not every day, of course... that would have been weird, and any girlfriend would have been fully within their rights to question that. But often: a single day at first and rising to three or four days a week when we realised we shared similar tastes in entertainment. Particularly comedy – which would lead to our various cannibal encounters.

But that still lay in the future.

Back to his girlfriend.

Cody offered to introduce us a bunch of times, but I always put him off at first, feeling that the two parts of his life should be kept separate. Perhaps scared that my bad luck would somehow curse what he had going with his partner.

Silly, I guess, looking back.

But to be expected.

For my luck had indeed turned bad these last few years.

Take this, for an example:

A group interview – forty people here – all sorts of ages. Men and women. Split into eight groups of five. Performing group-bonding exercises.

Make that weird *group-bonding exercises.*

The glass in front of me drops from the table, shatters on the floor.

The guy who's leading the interview – guy called Kelvin – looks at me.

"You... you were supposed to build something that could support the weight of the glass," he tells me. "Using the items provided."

Yes, indeed. How very true. Said items a couple of paper plates, some straws and some chewing gum. Something my hands could not do. And somewhere I can hear my old D.T. teacher laughing. Calling me "Jimmy" all the while.

I don't get the job.

Nor, I assume, do any of the other people in my group. Like I said before: cursed by my bad luck.

But, you know, looking down at the shattered glass, I can't help but wonder...

How is an exercise like this supposed to show that you'd be good at working at the cinema?

Answers on a postcard, please.

That would have been nice.

But what *actually* arrived in the electronic post, a few days after we'd put up our twelfth video, was anything *but* nice.

We had an e-mail address at the bottom of our page where you could get in touch with us – and, unlike a lot of the big-time vloggers, I bet, we actually tended to it ourselves. Which was just as well, considering what came in that day.

"It's from our old pal Cannibal Ken," Cody told me.

"Yeah." I looked over his shoulder at the computer screen. "He ever e-mailed us before?"

"Nah," Cody replied. "But he's a frequent commenter."

That much I knew already. The viewer who called himself Cannibal Ken had turned up after our second video, always complimenting us on how real our body parts looked, often getting into flame wars with viewers who said that they did not. In all that time, it had never occurred to me to ask just *how* he knew our stuff was so accurate. But now, seeing the name of the attachment he had sent us, I suddenly wasn't so sure that I wanted to open it, fan of us or not.

50

Real Live Flesh-Eating! it said.

"Come on," Cody said, trying to reassure me, obviously seeing the worry on my face. "He's just joking with us."

But the man called Cannibal Ken was not.

For when Cody pressed "play" on the video...

There was a man chained to a huge banquet-style table, manacled at the wrists and ankles.

He was almost naked.

All he wore was a big chef's hat.

He thrashed about furiously, but he could not break free. And all around him, masked men and women polished up knives and forks, looking at the body.

The men and women were dressed up as if for a party.

In fact, I could not help but notice just how good the women looked – wearing dresses that revealed long legs and high cleavage.

It had been a while for me, remember.

But when they started jabbing forks into the man, and when he started to scream, all thoughts of desire ran out of my mind.

The video cut off then, thankfully.

But just as I was about to ask Cody what he thought we should do, an odd thing happened.

The mail started to delete itself from our inbox.

"Shit, man," I said to my friend, panicking. "What's happening?"

He said nothing.

Just shook his head as the message erased itself from our e-mail trash can. Gone forever.

"Some sort of virus," he eventually explained. "I guess. So we couldn't show the video to anyone else."

An explanation which brought to mind images of tapes auto-destructing in all those old secret agent TV

51

shows. But this was nowhere near as entertaining as that. For I was sure that what we had just seen was one hundred per cent real.

"I think we'd best keep an eye on our old pal Cannibal Ken," Cody suggested.

But it turned out he'd been keeping eyes on us.

I'll get to how we came up with the cannibal idea in a little while... but first I want to tell you a little bit more about Cody and me. Including how I finally got to meet his girlfriend, Cecelia.

We never really argued about anything – but we came close to it a couple of times when talking about her. More specifically, my reluctance to meet the woman.

It came to a head when he got us tickets for a stand-up comedy show – an anthology one, over a dozen jokers in attendance.

"Are people on benefits allowed to spend their money on stuff like that?" I asked, smiling.

"Ha!" he replied, laughing back over the phone at me. "Nice call-back."

And call-backs to old jokes were something we would see plenty of at the show, many of our favourite comedians using them.

But I suddenly didn't feel so much like laughing when Cody's tone turned serious and he said, "Cecelia will be there, too."

"Oh," I said.

"Is that going to be a problem?"

I took a second to think about it before replying.

Truth to tell, I'd grown a lot more curious about his girlfriend in the last few months that we'd been friends. He talked about her so much that it was hard not to wonder what she was really like, the need to put a face to the mental picture I'd built up increasingly great. But the thought that I might be some sort of jinx still loomed large in my mind, obliterating all logic and reason whenever I tried to dispel it.

"But isn't it like..." I took a breath, tried again. "Won't it be like a date for you guys?"

"Not really," Cody said. "Just three friends having a night out together."

"We're not friends yet," I pointed out. "Me and Cecelia, I mean."

"So, give her a chance to change that."

I was wavering, I'll admit it.

But then, what was my only other option if I *didn't* go?

Sit around the house alone? Again? Bored and lonely when I could be out there having a laugh with other people? And just what the hell was wrong with me, anyway? I mean, what sort of a person at my age believed in jinxes and curses, right?

Right.

"Okay," I eventually said. "I'm in."

"Great!" he said, and I could hear both the smile and the relief in his voice. "Want me to bring one of Cecelia's friends along for you?"

"Don't push it," I told him.

"All right, all right," he replied. "No chickening out, mind."

I didn't.

I went along and I had great fun, and I have to say it: Cecelia wasn't at all like I expected her to be.

In an odd way, she sort of looked a little like Cody. Not in a physical way, though... there was nothing masculine about her at all, not in that dress she was wearing. No, it was something similar in the way they stood next to each other as I approached them – tall and proud and strong, facing the world head on.

"Hey," she said, squeezing my arm as I reached them, the hint of an Australian accent gone UK native in her voice. "Nice to finally meet you."

"Yeah," I said, smiling at her. "Sorry about that."

She gave me a wide-eyed stare. "Sorry? What for?"

"Ah, don't mind James." Cody shook his head at me, suggesting he had not told Cecelia about my reasons for not wanting to meet her. "He's always apologising for something."

"Not like *you*, then," she said, looking back to Cody.

And I could not help it: I laughed.

The first time of many that night, as the comedy show soon got underway.

But what I'll always remember of my first meeting with Cecelia is grabbing coffees in a bar afterwards. Talking with the two of them like we were all old friends. Hearing about how they'd met at a speed-dating event, how they'd lived together for two years, how she'd been there for Cody when he'd lost his job at the manufacturing site. It made me think unfavourably of my own ex-girlfriend, who'd left as soon as the money started to run out.

But sitting there with these people, it struck me that it was time to stop moping about. To stop thinking that I was cursed, or *a* curse, one inflicted on others. I started to think about moving to a new place in my life. One with preferably more money.

But that meant getting a job.

Which, of course, leads to:

Another interview.

This time for a burger restaurant.

The interviews held in a fancy hotel. A hotel where the toilet is bigger than my whole front room. I know this because I'm in there nervous, guts going crazy, shitting copious amounts of faecal matter into the cubicle. And I know why I'm so worked-up: I'm terrified of going back to the Job Place. Dreading the thought of being sent on one more awful course.

My Employment Advisor's patronising face floating in my mind.

"You've been unemployed for quite some time, James."

Turning over the pages of my employment logbook, where I write down every job that I've applied for. It's like he's doing it in slow motion. Judging my futile efforts as I sit and squirm before him.

"Have you looked for work this week, James?"

Like he can't see the answers spread out there before him.

Like Cody and I have done anything other than look for jobs all week.

That in mind, I'm pumped when I get out of the toilet, and I'm powering through the interview... another group one, but no stupid things to try and build this time, just a couple of ice-breaker questions like what's your name, what would you be if you were an item of food. I choose potato, because I saw a film about a killer potato once, and it's the first thing that springs to mind, and it gets a couple of laughs from the three people that are holding the interview, two men and a woman. So I'm thinking that all is good by the time we're taken out of the room into a hallway of the hotel for one-to-one interviews with the people from the burger place. Especially when I get the girl part of the trio.

But then she drops the bombshell.

"Well," she says, "it's actually a zero-hours contract we'd be offering you if you got the job..."

And she says more.

But I don't hear the rest.

A zero-hours contract.

So you could go whole weeks without getting any work from them.

Without getting any pay.

Without making any money.

In other words, a con.

Welcome to Conservative Britain 2017.

I start babbling about anything after that, talking the woman's ear off, trying to do anything to make them not give me the job without being too obvious about it. I don't want her feeding back to the Job Place, to my slimy-faced Employment Advisor, that I don't want a job. And at the same time I don't want them to offer me a job and then have to turn it down. Because the Job Place don't care if all you've got is a zero-hours contract. Just so long as you're off of their statistics book.

And I guess I get a little overexcited, a little loud.

Because that's when a man in his sixties comes out of the room we're sat next to, looks at me disapprovingly.

"Can you keep your voice down, son?" he asks. "I'm trying to teach a class in here."

Then walks off, tutting and shaking his head.

I look back to the interviewer.

Neither of us seem to know what to say.

"Well," she tries, and looks down at the clipboard in her hands. "Thanks for coming, James. We'll be in touch soon."

But I really hope they won't.

"So how'd it go?"

Cody was waiting at my place when I got back. I'd given him my spare key a month or so ago, the key left on the table by my ex-girlfriend when she headed out of there for the last time. Which might sound odd. But I trusted the guy. And really I had nothing that anyone would want to steal.

"Lame," I replied, and told him the whole thing. Including the unsmiling teacher.

"Cheeky twat," he said.

"Yeah," I said. I grabbed a can of lager from the fridge, decided to treat myself given the poor performance of this morning. "I'd like to put *him* into a burger."

Then I sat down on the couch next to Cody, motioned with my free hand to the computer screen before him.

"What you doing?" I asked. I cracked open the lager, took a sip, found that it was good. "Another job search?"

"I've been doing that all morning," he said. "I'm taking a little time off."

And watching online videos, I saw.

We did a lot of that, too. Often in an "ironic" way, though – watching things so we could mock them. And one thing that hours of endless day between pointless job interviews and equally pointless trips to the Job Place had taught us was that people could and did vlog about absolutely anything, the Internet having supplanted reality TV docu-soaps as the premier way for the completely talentless to court attention.

Take these three girls, as an example:

"Hi! I'm Kendra! And I'm going to show *you* how to paint your nails."

"Hi! I'm Sophie! And I'm going to show *you* how to apply your make-up."

"Hi! I'm Sandra! And I'm going to show *you* how to wipe your ass . . ."

See what I mean?

"These suck," Cody said.

"Agreed." I took the last swig from my can. "When did the Internet become just people showing you how to do stuff?"

"Not just stuff," he pointed out. "Stuff that's just common sense for everyone."

"Yeah."

He grinned. "I'd rather have one that showed me how to make a guy into a burger."

"Ha!" I toasted him with my empty can. "Nice callback."

But he had sudden glint in his eye as he looked back at me.

"What?" I said. "What is it?"

"How'd you like to make a vlog of our own?" he asked.

Thus was born the Cannibal Cooking Channel – Cody mostly on filming duties whilst I portrayed the Chef.

The body parts we put together from cardboard, Papier-Mache, whatever we could get our hands on – and, since we lived near an area well-known for fly-tipping, that was usually plenty. I'd paint them up from tins I had kicking around since the last time I tried to decorate – which, again, I had a lot of, since it had really been my ex-girlfriend that had wanted to spruce up the place, and she hadn't really done a lot of that before disappearing. And I have to admit it, they looked pretty good. Not enough to make Internet police think they were genuine, but I still thought they were rather cool.

Next came the camera we used to film our videos. Cecelia loaned Cody the money to buy it, and I went along to the shop with them to pick it up.

"Don't you mind him spending money on this?" I asked her, putting the question to her discreetly whilst Cody was up at the counter, paying for the item in question. "When he's on Job Find benefits, I mean."

"Guys always have their little hobbies," she replied. Then looked to her partner, affection in her eyes. "I know he'll pay me back when he can. And if it keeps him happy 'til then..."

And it did.

The two of us had great fun.

I read somewhere that a lot of classic TV comedies were written by pairs, and one of the reasons those shows were so successful was that the writers were always trying to make each other laugh, to outdo whatever their writing partners had come up with. And working on the videos those few months, I could well believe it. We had a great time grossing one another out with new human meal ideas – Toe Pie, the ever-popular Knuckle Sandwich – and we steadily watched our viewership grow, and loved every minute. It wasn't until that twelfth video that I realised discontent had started to set in.

Cody asked me about it, once we'd put the camera away for the day.

"What's up, bud?" he asked.

"Ah, it's nothing," I said. I looked at my watch. "Go on, get out of here. It's almost teatime. Cecelia will be waiting for you."

But he crossed his arms in front of him, resolute in the middle of the room.

"Not until you tell me what's wrong," he insisted.

I sank back into the couch, sighed.

"It's just... where are we going with this vlog thing, Cody?"

"Going?" He shrugged. "We're having fun with it,

James. Why does it have to *go* anywhere?"

I nodded, seeing the sense in his words.

But as he grabbed his coat and left, telling me to call him if I needed to, I found myself chewing over what he had said.

I supposed that he was right. I mean, we had started the Cannibal Cooking Channel as a laugh, never intending it to go anywhere, certainly not with the idea of it making us any money. But all those comments, all those likes, all those virtual fans... it just seemed like it should *mean* something, you know? Yet still here we sat between videos, claiming benefits, finding no work. Going nowhere.

But that was the way I'd always been. I'd never been much good at living in the moment, unable to appreciate the here and now. Everything had to be building to something further at all times. There had to a progression. Even with the girls I had known, the ones I had been with. A date was never just a date, no matter how great it had been. I constantly wondered, *where next?*

Probably why they always left me.

I guess that was kind of hard for them to take.

Sighing at this realisation, wishing it had come a whole lot sooner, when I could have done something about it to stop them leaving, I decided to have myself an early night.

The next day we got our first video from Cannibal Ken.

The day after that...

I met my new girlfriend.

Looking back, I guess it's obvious the two things were linked, coming so close to each other. At the time, though, I truly never noticed... I was just glad for the female attention.

She came up to me whilst I was sitting outside of the Job Place.

"Going in?" she said. "Or coming out?"

I looked up at her.

It wasn't a jaw-dropping movie moment or anything like that. That's not the way I am – in fact, I'd been friends with all of my previous partners for years before becoming romantically involved with them, the kind of guy who likes to wait for something there to grow. But I'm also the type of guy that never looks a gift horse in the mouth, so I flashed her a charming smile and said, "Going in. Planning on it, anyway."

She smiled back.

It struck me that she looked like she really did not belong there.

There was something elegant about her. Something fancy, though I could not quite put my finger on whatever it was.

She glanced around herself nervously then, as if getting ready to share some great secret. "This is my first time here."

Could I remember mine?

I wasn't sure.

"Damn," I said to her, shaking my head. "Good luck."

And I thought that would be that.

But then she sat down next to me.

Said, "Look, I know this is odd, but I'm really scared." Then locked her eyes on mine, digging deep into me, or so it seemed. "Would you... would you wait for me?" She moved her gaze away, a slightly shy look on her face. "Then maybe we could do something after I'm done? Would you mind?"

Would I mind?

Hell, no.

Well, if I was being honest, I would have told her I had nothing better to do, since my friend Cody was off at an interview. But where's the romance in that?

"Of course not," I told her.

"Thanks." She held out a hand. "I'm Alice."

"James," I said, taking her hand. "Pleased to meet you."

And was that trip to the Job Place a little less soul-crushing than usual? Oh yes. And did I wait for her, as promised? Indeed. And did we spend a great afternoon together after that? Well...

Let me fill you in as I tell Cody and Cecelia.

"You pulled at the Job Place?"

This was round at their house. They were treating me to tea. And all around the table Cecelia had laid out little plastic placards, on which were printed the names of some of the meals we'd concocted for our channel. I particularly liked the one marked "Vlog's Legs," invented about a vlogger we especially hated called Justin. A very nice touch, I'm sure you'll agree.

"Yep," I told Cody. "Well, outside of it, you know?"

"Ha!" Cody said. I was only now starting to notice how much we both liked that exclamation. "You sure she's not a zombie?"

I'm not sure why, but that comment made me flash back to the video we'd been sent.

I shivered.

Luckily, though, Cecelia came to the rescue, play-punching Cody's shoulder, saying, "Leave him alone, you." Then looking to me. "I'm happy for you, James.

When are you supposed to be seeing her again?"

"Friday," I said.

But it would turn out to be sooner than that.

Much sooner.

For she was waiting outside my house when I arrived.

I was bloated by then, having stuffed myself with Cecelia's awesome home-cooked food. But still, seeing Alice standing there, I was tempted to turn and run – I mean, I hadn't told her where I lived... so how could she be here?

But here indeed she was.

And I lost the chance to run away when she saw me, beckoned me over.

She had changed since the afternoon, I saw. She'd been in casual clothes then, not even wearing any make-up. But now she was dressed for the night, wearing tights, high boots, and a thick black coat that covered her from neck to thigh. And I have to say she looked good.

"Alice?" I said, coming over to her. "What are you doing here?"

"Waiting for you," she replied. And nodded her head back towards my house, a slight smile on her lips. "Aren't you going to invite me in?"

I probably shouldn't have done.

But I did.

"Yes," I told her. "Of course."

"Good." She smiled. "I thought you would."

And she placed her hand on mine.

And soon we were kissing as we made our way into my house, and naturally she did not have anything on beneath that coat. Just the tights and the boots and a whole lot of skin. And soon just the skin, and as we headed into my bedroom I hoped that this was really happening, that it was not all some sort of dream. Or worse, that Alice was merely an escort, one that Cody had hired to sort me out...

A thought that vanished from my mind when she lay naked on the bed beneath me, me crouched above her, ready to enter her, and she looked up at me and said:

"Eat me."

I looked down at the moistness of her opening, still wet from my mouth. "I thought I just had..."

"Not like that." Her gaze grew feverish, intense. "My flesh, I mean. Eat my flesh."

Oh God, I thought.

Was this another crazy fan?

Another Cannibal Ken, someone who thought our vlogs were all for real?

As if sensing my thoughts, Alice said, "You *are* the guy from the Cannibal Cooking Channel, right?"

My erection was starting to wilt.

My mind starting to think about jinxes and curses once more.

"Yeah," I said. "But that's all just a joke, Alice. None of it is real."

I thought this would disappoint her.

That she would now pull on her clothes and then leave.

But she was nodding even before I finished speaking.

"Good," she said. "You pass the test. Now kiss me."

I hesitated.

But then she did something that stopped my erection from wilting.

And we put it to good use.

"Alice," I moaned into the soft flesh of her neck as we did so. "Oh, Alice . . ."

"That's good," she moaned back, body now rocking with mine, building up a steady rhythm that suited us both. "But my name's not Alice."

I was about to ask her what she meant.

But then her lips found mine.

And stayed there sucking, sometimes biting, until we both were done.

After that I was exhausted and fell into a sleep almost deep enough to be labelled as passing-out. But kept my arm around Alice all night, perhaps scared that she would disappear on me like all the other women I had been with throughout the years.

But I failed in this task, as in most others.

She was gone when I woke up.

I sighed.

Well, it's not for the first time, I thought. *And it probably won't be the last.* Though I was already dreading telling Cody and Cecelia. They'd be so *disappointed* for me...

Then I rolled onto the other side.

And gasped.

There was a man standing in the corner of the room.

I leapt up onto my feet, crying, "Who the hell are you?" Subconsciously balling my hands into fists, getting ready for a fight.

"Relax," he said, patting the air in front of him for calm.

I wasn't ready to be calm yet. But I was cooling enough to look him over, and I saw that, though he appeared to be in his mid-forties, he was a hell of a lot better built than I was, firm at the chest and arms. In fact, he looked like he could eat me up for breakfast, no matter *how* tense my fists currently were.

"What are you..." I glanced around my room, wondered if I'd just dreamt the night before. "What are you doing here?"

"I'm here to take you to Abigail," he said.

"Who?"

"I believe you know her as Alice."

I remembered what she'd said about her name a few hours earlier. "And where is she?"

"Gone to get your good friend Cody," the man said. "Along with a few of the other members of our club."

"Club?" I said. "You're not making any sense." I sat down on the edge of the bed, let the tension drain from my fists, let them become just hands once more. "Why don't you just tell me who you are?"

And has the penny dropped yet?

"You probably know me as Cannibal Ken." He stepped forward, placed a rough hand upon my bare shoulder. "And now I'd like for you to come with me."

I did so.

What choice did I have?

If it had just been me, I might not have obeyed, might have even tried to fight him. But the guy had mentioned Cody, too. And there was no way I could ignore that.

So I got dressed and I followed him out of the house.

I had no idea where we were going. Given the bizarreness of the way that we had met, though – not to mention the fact that I now knew he was the man behind the awful video we'd been sent – I was expecting our destination to be some grotty abandoned factory. Where he could kill and eat me in peace.

But if that were his aim, why had he not yet done so?

And why would he defend us so vehemently on our Channel's page?

I wanted answers.

So I tried to ask him questions along the way.

But he would give me nothing.

Merely saying, "You'll find out when we get there."

The "there" in question still a mystery to me.

But then we reached it.

It wasn't an abandoned factory.

But I was close.

It was a derelict high-rise office block.

"This way," Cannibal Ken said.

Then led me around to the back of the building, where he pushed open a dirty door with cracks in it.

I followed him through.

Into the cracked and dirty remains of a reception area.

"One of the members of our club is always on the lookout for dead places," he explained as we walked. "Today it's this one. Next month when we meet, it will be another."

I was about to ask him to expand on that one.

But then something else caught my attention.

Voices.

Lots of them.

Coming from the other side of a door that lay just in front of us.

I looked to Cannibal Ken.

He nodded.

And I placed my hand upon the door.

Pushed.

And saw...

Masked men and women.

Dozens of them.

Just like on the video.

And in the middle of them, strapped up to a chair, was Cody.

I looked back to Ken, entering the room behind me.

"If you've done anything to hurt my friend..." I said.

Actually, I wasn't sure how to complete that sentence. But Ken made it unnecessary, saying, "Of course we haven't. It's just your colleague needed a little extra prompting to stay here."

Meaning he had something to go back home to.

Unlike me.

"Well, you can let him go now," I said.

Hearing me, Ken nodded to one of the many masked men within the room.

The man stepped forward, withdrew a knife from his pocket, cut through the ropes that had held Cody.

Freed, my friend leapt up, looked to me, said, "James?"

I walked over to him.

"James," he said again. "What's going on here? These guys grabbed me from my house when Cecelia had left for work, they –"

"Relax," I told him, smiling, laying a hand upon his shoulder.

Then I looked around the room.

The men and women were all dressed the same, just like in the video – men in suits, women in dresses. And the masks made it impossible to tell them apart. So I tried something else.

"Alice?" I said. "Or is it Abigail?"

And she stepped forward.

Removed her mask.

"Alice was the name I used at the Job Place," she explained. "So I could meet you."

"But why?"

"We've been watching you for a while," she went on. "We knew when you'd be there. I set up a claim under a false name, organised it so I'd have my meeting there on the same day as you."

I thought back to our meeting.

I saw it all now.

How could I have been so blind?

"So none of it was real?" I said.

She smiled.

"It wasn't *supposed* to be," she replied.

And for a moment I lost myself in her words, in her eyes.

Wondering, could there ever be something between us, when our first meeting had been based around a lie?

I didn't know.

But before I could find an answer, another door swung open.

And they brought the armless, legless man in. Strapped to a hospital stretcher.

Beside me, Cody gasped.

Said, "That's –"

"I know."

It was the man from the video.

The one who'd been bound to the table, the one wearing the chef's hat.

"Our former chef," Ken explained, coming up behind us. Then he looked around the rest of the club. "Everybody out!" he ordered. "Everybody except you, Abigail."

They obeyed.

Leaving the four of us alone.

And the man on the stretcher, of course.

"Why former?" Cody asked, looking down at him.

"He broke the number one rule of our club," Ken replied.

"Which is?"

"The chef must not eat of the flesh he cooks."

"That was why I tested you last night," Abigail explained. "I had to make sure you did not want to eat me."

"What's she talking about, James?" Cody wondered.

"Simple," I said, and I looked up at Ken. "I think this is an interview, right?"

Ken nodded.

Abigail took a step closer, laid her hand on mine.

I let her.

I liked the way it felt there.

I wanted it to stay a long time.

"We knew your videos were just a joke," Ken continued. "Of course we did. But in your humour, we saw something else. We saw potential. So when we realised our chef was breaking our rules..."

"We made a little video," Abigail added. "Did you like the little extra I added, so you couldn't forward it on to anyone else?"

I looked to her. "That was you?"

She nodded. "I found out where you lived, too. Easy to do once we had your e-mail address."

"Wow," I said, impressed.

"I'm not just a pretty face," she said, and there was something hungry in her voice. Something that made my penis pulse once more, wanting her.

Shaking my head, not sure what I was feeling, I glanced down at the one-time chef.

He was still alive.

Barely.

His arms and legs had been severed but had then been stitched quite well.

"One of our club is a surgeon of some success," Ken explained.

I nodded.

Finding myself looking the man over the way I used to when we were planning out a fake meal on our channel. Wondering what we could do with the body parts he had left. And all the juicy organs still beneath his skin...

I blinked.

But the image remained.

"What do you think?" I then said to Cody.

He had eyes on the man, too.

The quivering, blubbery man. All that flesh. And what fun, I was thinking, what such fun we could have with it...

"You can't be serious," Cody said. But I could tell that it was half-hearted on his part, a token protest. "I mean, what'll I tell Cecelia?"

"You'll think of something," I replied.

"He's right." Ken stepped forward, put an arm around our shoulders. "And remember, the chef here is a special case. Normally, we only eat the worst people in society – murderers, rapists, Tory voters..."

"I get it," I said, and I did. I finally did.

The video had been sent to test us – to see what we would do. Then Ken and Abigail had started watching us – wanting to see if we started to freak out, I suppose. When we hadn't, that was when they'd moved in.

Now, I only had one question for them.

"And you'll pay us?" I said.

Ken laughed. "Of course."

Cody looked to me.

I could tell what he was thinking.

He confirmed it, saying, "So we could come off benefits?"

"Naturally," Ken told us. "Not under your official

club title, which will be "Executive Menu Officers." But we'll call you a P.A. or something like that. We'll make it work."

"We always do," Abigail put in.

I realised her hand was still on mine.

And I knew that what we had was real.

I smiled, feeling happy for the first time in... well, who can remember?

"We're in," I told Ken. "But give us a minute here, all right?"

He bowed and then obeyed, Abigail leaving, too, shooting me one last longing look that made me ache to bed her once again.

But all in time.

First things first.

For now, I looked to Cody.

"Hey," I said. "You know what this means?"

But from the sudden tears leaking from his eyes I could tell that he did.

No more Job Place.

We were employed again.

THE CAPSULE
David A. Sutton

I'm fifty-seven years old. It's an estimate. And cheerless as cold moorland granite. I can see my wife Anna from where I am standing in the lounge and her features, framed by her unchanging gorgeous blonde hair, are as sad as mine. She's sat at the breakfast room table, staring in my direction, or into space. And I wonder if, like me, she is dwelling on the unfulfilled past. Our shared one, or another.

I remember the Jug o' Punch Folk Club in the sixties. This was Ian Campbell's venue in Birmingham, at the Digbeth Civic Hall near the city centre. I'd meet my friends there and go for a madras curry up the road at the Manzil afterwards to sober up. Late on in the evening the Jug o' Punch would be smoky and noisy, and the floor would be swimming in beer and cider. I mean literally swimming. I don't ever remember there being any trouble at the Jug. You'd have a drink and a sing-along and there'd be resident folk singers and guest singers and Ian Campbell would encapsulate the proceedings with his group. With all the swaggering about a lot of drink got spilled.

I was at the bar buying three pints of cider, for me, Paddy and Ray. It was an unusually quiet moment, but there was one young chap standing there, nursing a half pint of the scrumpy. He neither looked the type to drink that brew or the kind to frequent folk clubs. But there was no accounting for taste. For instance, I was starting to look scruffy and a bit alternative; next year I'd be a hippy. This chap looked like an ultra-spivvy Mod, left over from the last decade. For a second I thought he might be a ponce. But with his greased black hair and pale skin... well, he looked like a stranger to sunlight.

"Hello," he said as I placed my order with the barman.

He had to be speaking to me, so I had to reply, but he was weird. "Hello," I replied. "Good music tonight," I added just to say something. It was actually pretty average.

"Are you with someone?" the man asked. At that point the barman put the third pint of scrumpy on the counter, so it was pretty obvious I was.

"Friends." I'd met Paddy at the shop where I was based as area stock-taker. He'd teamed up with Ray after he left selling shoes to find employment with the credit reference agency Ray worked at. And the three of us had become firm friends. We all hated our jobs, which was a focus for our rebelliousness.

"Is this..." the weird one said, changing his angle of approach. "Is this good music?" Man, I thought, escape plan B required.

"Depends," I replied evenly, before thinking, what do I know? It's a matter of preference. Some nights are good, some not so. It was then I noticed that the man's posture was stiff, as if he was uncomfortable being there, or found it difficult to remain standing. Maybe he was an undercover policeman looking for drug deals. "What sort of folk music do you like?" I asked, trying to extricate his tastes. Why else was he here? Well, yes ok, there were plenty of other reasons, I suppose, but folk music of one sort or another was the foremost reason you frequented the club.

He didn't answer. I paid the barman and started to pick up the drinks. "Better get these delivered," I said, not wanting to prolong the conversation.

"I have something…" When the barman's back was turned he placed a capsule on the bar towel.

"Sorry, I'll stick to the cider, if you don't mind."

"Take it," the man said hurriedly. "I have to go. This," he pointed a pale, bony finger at the all-black coloured pill, "will change everything." Then he walked out of the club without a backward glance. Fuck, I thought, trick or treat — it could be either, or both. It was Halloween, after all. And he might well have been a stand-in for Dracula.

I carefully replaced the three pint glasses that I was balancing and picked up the capsule. It was warm to the touch, but other than that looked innocuous enough. I slipped it into the pocket of my corduroy jacket before the barman noticed. Ray and Paddy were often travelling to London, where they'd score some speed and buy tickets to Ronnie Scott's, and for the rest of the weekend would live at high velocity. I wasn't ready for that yet, but not so far off tripping the light fantastic. I really thought that pot and beer were all I needed, but as it was, mixing weed and alcohol made me nauseous and green anyway, so I wasn't particularly interested in varying my own personal pharmacopoeia just then. Besides, the weird guy had *given* me the capsule, not even attempted to sell it. If that was some new ploy to get you hooked on something, I thought, it's not going to work.

At home late that night I was still savouring the curry the three of us had eaten. My stomach kept reminding me. I needed another kind of fix — liver salts.

I met *him* again at the Jug o' Punch the following week. I was on my own this time and we began to chat. He was still wacky, but I kept telling myself that I was moving in that direction too. Stuff had happened. The folk scene was still a draw, but not as much as it used to be. I'd been listening to Soft Machine and Zappa; Pink Floyd had gigged at the Town Hall and I'd set the controls for the heart of the sun.

It was during the interval between sets and I was at the bar chatting — if that's what you could call the bizarre conversation — to Nigel. That was his name. At least that's what he told me, though the way he introduced himself I had my doubts.

"That pill," I finally got around to saying.

"You didn't take it." It was a statement.

I felt that the comment didn't need an answer anyway, I mean, who would take a sweetie from a stranger? Even on All Hallows Eve.

"Do you still have it?" he asked, and I nodded.

"Would you like it back?" I don't know why, but the night after I'd come into possession of the capsule, I put it in a drawer in my bed-sit where I kept my pens, pencils and typewriter paper. The capsule was unusual, not like anything I'd seen before. Well, yes, sort of like flu remedy medicine, but it was very slim and jet-black in colour and had nothing printed on it to say what it was.

"No. But you mustn't throw it away. I should have said last time. It's the only one left." Nigel said this in such a curious way, part longing and part regret on his face. As if he had sought an answer that I could've given him, had I ingested the 'medicine'. He swept the long fringe of black hair that half shielded his eyes back, with a weary gesture. His eyes were sunk in, and gleamed with reflected light; his skin was almost translucent. Even in the semi-darkness of the club I imagined I could see his cheekbones and the skeletal grimace of his teeth through the skin. He appeared to be immensely tired.

I consumed half my glass of cider. The buzz from fermented apples was seriously better than lager. And I was feeling that buzz after two pints. "I'm sure you can get more where they came from," I said flippantly. I was waiting for him to plead for money to buy his next fix.

Nigel looked at me seriously. "*No*," he insisted. "It really is the only one left... in the world. As far as I'm aware."

I began to think he was having me on. A little joke; Halloween last week, remember. I didn't respond immediately but looked hard at him. It wasn't embarrassing, because his face was turned slightly away, in profile. He was leaning with his back against the bar, looking towards the stage with a half-focused stare. I think he was older than I'd first thought. I'd taken him for a bit of a leftover Mod the first time I'd seen him, but now I wasn't so sure. Though he was wearing a parka that night, yet it was as if it didn't suit him, as if he was unsuited to a role that wasn't him. Perhaps because the club was steaming the thermometer's mercury, he looked uncomfortable. The parka, I reflected oddly, was a costume; on him it resembled a cowl with bat wings. I was wearing jeans and a tie-dyed vest and I was sweating hot.

He was unconnected somehow. It's difficult to explain. His demeanour, his face with its faraway look. I don't know... Sometimes his eyes would lose focus as if he found it impossible to concentrate for more than a minute or two. He was searching for something perhaps. Like me he was seeking meaning to life. The psychic bullet that I too had pursued, that would end my adolescent tensions and explain the universe. I'd vicariously had spiritual journeys and Faculty X and Jung and Koestler, but the books were only a temporary patch-up. The search went on.

"I think I'd better go." Nigel caught me staring at him.

"Sorry —"

"No. It's all right," Nigel said. "The music's back on in a minute." He slumped down into his parka as if defeated. "I can't tell if it's good or not."

There he goes again, I thought. It's as if he had been living on a different planet. "It's good – if you like a sing-a-long," I answered. "Don't take it too seriously." Even the protest songs were fun to listen to, if you got into the crowd mojo.

"Still…"

"Wait," I demanded. "About that capsule." I was intrigued and decided I needed to know more. But I was finding it hard myself to concentrate. I was half drunk. Then he said something that made me think that he *was* from another planet. The one where you invited in the men in white coats. Not the ones from the chemistry lab.

"Where did I get it? What's in it? What's it do?" He shrugged. "I can't answer all of those questions, if that's what you were going to ask. I can tell you how I got the one I took and the one you have."

I ordered another pint of cider and nodded at Nigel's near empty glass. He declined, shaking his head. As the barman allowed the yellow liquid to drain out of a barrel behind the bar I waited for Nigel to speak.

The audience were beginning to stir and cheer as the guest band started to return to the stage, and Nigel had to raise his voice to make himself heard.

"My dad and me were driving home from Leicester one night. A couple," he hesitated as if the word 'couple' may have been an estimate, "of years ago. It was a regular trip for us. Then we both started to have sleeping problems and anxiety attacks. I discovered the capsules in my pocket afterwards and was puzzled how they got there, but just kept them anyway. Then Dad and I tried to figure out what had happened that night. He worked out that during the journey home we'd *lost* two hours."

I knew what was coming. I'd read about such things before, quite recently.

"I mean, the journey was run of the mill, yet it took two hours *more* than expected to reach home." Nigel paused, but if he was expecting me to be amazed, he was deluded.

He gestured and moved out into the vestibule of the civic hall. It was a lot quieter out there. I followed, still with my pint in my hand. You never left an unfinished drink in the Jug — it would end up on the floor.

"And you'd been abducted by aliens," I said, trying not to smirk.

"There was some sort of contact, yes," he answered seriously. "Everything was hazy. I don't live with Dad and Mum anymore. Things became difficult. I was given the capsules that night. Eventually I took one." Nigel spoke quickly, this was a confession he'd obviously never made to anyone else.

I think he took offence at me making light of his close encounter of the third kind, because suddenly he took off, leaving me with my true companion, my scrumpy cider, and looking like I'd been stood up.

The question that shook me, really, was why had he given *me* the other capsule? I didn't believe he'd been prescribed black capsules by a little green man, but even if it was, say, a pill for flu, why? What did it mean? Yes, there are sad people out there. I'd always been pretty open-minded. Yet I do not know why Nigel was spooking me. Spooking me in his absence now. Perhaps I'd been listening to too much Gong and Third Ear Band.

*

I swallowed the capsule late one night a few weeks later. I'd been out drinking with Paddy and Ray; we'd been discussing putting together an underground magazine. I'd be printing it on my newly acquired ink duplicator. Paddy was hanging on for the ride. I don't think he was as interested in the magazine as me and Ray. We were just his friends and good for a bosting night out. Ray was serious and intense. We'd joined CND, were reading *Oz* and *International Times* and *Private Eye* and both Ray and I were getting wild to have our own political views out there in the world.

After several pints of modified apple juice – possibly compromised by the addition of the landlord's piss — at The Greyhound on Holloway Head, and the obligatory madras at the Manzil, I arrived home steaming from the alcohol and high on plans for the mag: *Outside Review* it was going to be called. Life was starting to mean something. The 'zine would have reviews, poetry, and our incisive, angry diatribes against the world.

Once I'd struggled to find the light in the bed-sit, I hit a pint of flat cider from the fridge and popped the capsule in what I can only describe as a moment of madness. There was a slight plastic taste on my tongue and then it disappeared down my gullet. I waited for something to happen.

I'm fifty-seven years old. That's an approximation. There's been a disconnection. The sixties and seventies have come and gone and I'm showing very little for two decades of potential spiritual growth. Anna bore me two children, Richard and his younger sibling, Fran. Everything went all right for a while. If you assume bringing up a family in the Western mode is the correct way. I used to despise the way people so easily filled the mould that society and politicians prepared for them.

Outside Review would have berated the proles who succumbed. Then I, too, filled the mould like a runny blancmange.

Outside Review went to issue two before it — and my two political friends — departed. There's only so much you can do with limited resources and mine were being hampered by mortgage, children, and newly invented videocassette recorders.

I look at Anna now with a longing that's almost unbearable. Where has our time gone? Richard crushed his body in the car we bought for his seventeenth birthday. His promising university days as severed as his limbs. Our family sundered, three souls left treading water, gasping for air. Not long after, Fran, fuelled by drugs and discord, hit the metropolis and the game. At least she survived, if you count the desert of Western Australia as survival. She escaped at least.

And I stare at Anna, watching her sitting at the cold kitchen table. Outside the window, morning sunlight is streaming in, blazing on the tiles. Yet it's chilly. Her long, still-beautiful blonde hair is draping her face, concealing it. Her head is bent; she is looking at pages of photographs in an album. I can guess whose pictures they are. I approach her, and my hand involuntarily caresses her hair. She turns and looks up, distracted, her eyes shimmering with tears.

Trying to amalgamate my thoughts, everything returns to the night I digested the capsule. Life for me changed then. I think about Nigel, wonder what kind of creature he had become by the time I met him; demon or clownish Halloween vampire . . . There's something missing, some key element. Like close encounters and missing time. I'd had the time, yet I've missed the time. Years have elapsed, but some years have disappeared.

I think I am a married man in middle age; had and lost children to death and desertion. But I still have Anna, I have to believe that, even if she appears elusive. She acknowledges me I am sure, in some way, even though I am tempted to say that I feel ephemeral. As if, ever since that night, I have been the inhabitant of another body. An alien within me not quite in touch with the outer skin or the synapses in my brain. These sensations have been there for years, but short-lived until recently, like momentary light-headedness after sudden exercise, or as if I am a wraith rising on All Hallows Eve, a skeletal apparition, trying to find its way.

I watched as Anna stood and walked into the living room and put on one of my old LP's. The music soared, supernal. Yet I didn't experience the vibe, not in that old way. She'd cried as the last notes and the stereo went silent. She lifted the platter and returned it reverently to its sleeve, wiping away tears. Something like heartache constricted my chest.

I gazed at her across the room from the doorway, wondering why she'd played the record. I couldn't ask her. It may have been my birthday or an anniversary. I couldn't ask her you see. She hasn't really known me for some time. As if I wasn't there.

Was my experience better than that of a sparrow, sodden and diseased, hiding under a winter's hedge, waiting for hypothermia to bring an end? Or an old pet dog, behind the door, clammy and unconscious with toxic shock. Its owner out at work, the dog's unfettered love involuntarily spurned during its final hours. Beauty always meets horror at the end. When was ever our mortal race's termination a dignified one? Were we ever free from pain and anguish and squalid ills? I had no more answers now than I'd had in my youth.

The capsule's effect was cumulative, that much I knew. It merely needed time. I came to realise it didn't need reinforcement with ever increasing doses of the same. The content of the capsule was an entity working of its own volition. I should have faced up to what was happening years ago, but I hadn't. I dread facing up to reality now; it was never my strong point.

It's the thirty-first of October again, I suddenly realise. I think I am middle aged. I think I may be alive.

But it's impossible to tell.

WAKE UP SCREAMING
Adrian Cole

I reckon everyone gets realistic dreams. You only know they're dreams when you wake up. Sometimes it's disappointing. Others, you're glad to break free. And then there's the really nasty ones when you're shit-scared.

This one was like that. A real terror storm. My dream was about me, being asleep, when something climbed into the sheets with me. It groped for me. I beat at it with my hands. Tried to scream. You know how that is? Throat seems constricted, can't get any volume. Adds to the terror.

There was a feeling of being watched, like a bunch of huge crows were perched nearby, red eyes gleaming like jewels. Whatever the fuck they really were, one of them was the thing in the bed.

I got out a scream, a kind of bray. Ripped my way out of the dream. The guy I was in bed with had a hold of my wrists. Making a gurgling sound. Like he was maybe calling out to me that it was okay. I rolled over and stared at the darkness. It was like being at the bottom of the sea. Muttered an apology. The guy had already sunk back into his own dreams, asleep again in moments. I saw blurred things in the dark. Not huge crow-things. Just furniture. The flat was almost empty.

What the fuck? It had been a dream. What prompted it? Maybe the guy had rolled over and pressed up against me. Triggered the feeling of being groped. Maybe he was dreaming himself, reliving what we'd been doing earlier. It had been okay, but nothing special.

I turned to where I'd dropped my watch on the bedside table. The luminous numbers said 3.20 AM. Time to get out of there.

I got up and dressed in the dark. I splashed water on my face and rinsed my hands in the sink, all in near total darkness. Didn't want to wake the guy. He was of no further interest. I'd picked him up in the bar, one of several I'd looked over. Okay for the night. No more than that. I'm not ready for a steady relationship. Sex is okay, in its place.

Time to get going. I picked up my hessian shopping bag and looped it over a shoulder. I was on early starts this week, so I wasn't going to have time to go back to my flat, which was the other side of town. No problem. I had my work stuff in the bag.

I glanced at the heaped bedclothes, smeared in darkness. No regrets, end of. Left the flat, still in my Goth-black night gear and stilettos. Anonymously I went down the stairs, out into the still dark night and away. Tube was a fifteen-minute walk. Cold without a coat. Saw hardly anyone. Couple of drunks. One car rumbled by. Don't suppose anyone noticed me, wrapped in shadows. Suited me. I didn't want some nutter trying to get funny. The dream came back at me, like a sour after-taste.

I had a tube carriage to myself. Changed lines twice. Got to my stop with an hour to spare before work. Slipped into the toilets and changed into my work clothes. Long black hair piled up, tucked in under my white cap. Scraped off all the make-up. Pale face, gaunt. Meek little maid. Uniform, flat shoes. Real nonentity. That's how I like it.

Crammed the night clothes into the plastic bag and pulled it tight. Time to go into the day world, cog in the machine. Grind along. Earn some money, enough to live off. Forget about the night, its pleasures, its clammy dream. Tom, or Tony, whatever his name was, wouldn't remember me. I suppose he'd get up and go to his own day job. That was okay.

I went round the back of the restaurant, let myself in with my key and got to the kitchens, pretty much on time. Two other girls were drinking coffee from the machine. It was muck but it got you awake. I didn't need any. We all nodded to each other. They looked bushed. Clubbing until the early hours. At least I'd got some sleep.

Chef came in and growled his usual greeting. Got on with his preparations. We all had our own stuff to do, mostly menial work. I had some washing down to see to, so rolled up my sleeves, bare, white arms exposed. Skinny bitch, me. But no needle marks, no bruises. Fuck that game. I've seen enough walking corpses. I don't do drugs. Yeah, I drink, but not that much. Not enough to kill me.

Then the idiot came in, all fucking smiles. Dez. Still in his teens, six years younger than me, Knew it all. Funky, cocky, he was going places. Horny, sex on offer. In his fucking dreams. He worked out, as he told us all the time, though he was all skin and bone, under six feet, cropped hair, wet mouth. Sleazy little creep. Thought all the girls were panting for him. Like we owed him something.

"Morning, Joanie," he said to me. "How's my little mouse today?"

I gave him a sour smile. Just keep the fuck away from me, I wanted to add, trying to sharpen the message with my eyes.

He was a shifty bastard. Looked at Chef, who was busy, but wouldn't stand for any crap. He was a big guy, maybe forty, and I reckon he'd shape up well enough in a scuffle. Dez was too crafty to get funny with Chef, especially here.

"Get that bacon rolling," Chef called out and Dez jumped like he'd been slapped. He slid away from where I was still cleaning surfaces. I'd done them the evening before, but Chef liked everything gone over again in the mornings. The grease always clogged everything up, no matter how much you worked at it. It made the air thick and clammy. The floor was always slippery with it.

Later we had a coffee break. Chef did his usual and went out into the side alley to smoke. Dez brought me a cup of coffee. I needed it now, so took it, nodding my thanks.

"Thought any more about my offer?" he said. The girls and two other guys were bunched up further down the kitchen, laughing at some private joke. I didn't have a lot to do with them. Work was work. Play was for somewhere else.

"No offence, Dez, but I just don't want to."

"Hell, Joanie. You know I've got the hots for you. Just one date. I'm not going to eat you. What harm would it do?"

I shook my head. "I just want to be left alone."

"So what do you at night? Oh, yeah, you read. And watch movies. That's okay. I like movies. We can sit and watch movies."

While you slide your mucky hands over me, I thought. Not me, you scumball.

"Thanks all the same."

I could see his renewed frustration, and his anger. But he couldn't show it in the kitchen. Chef would be on him like a bear. No one was allowed to slack, or moan, or step out of line with Chef. Any trouble and you were out, quickly replaced. Chef was quick to tell us people were queuing up for our jobs.

Dez backed off, though I knew he'd be back. He was the sort who'd keep on pushing his luck until he got his way. Well, not with me.

In the afternoon, I was getting fish ready for the evening rush. We did a lot of fish. I cleaned them and filleted them. Chef said I had a knack for it. To me, it was just mechanical. I liked using the knife. Sharp, incisive. Stank a bit, which was probably why none of the others wanted the job. I scrubbed my arms hard afterwards. Always took ages to get rid of the stink. I'd finish it at home. I was going to be glad to get home, having been out all night.

Dez sidled up to me. Chef was upstairs, talking to management.

"Sure you won't come out with me?" he said, his white face creased in a smile, his tongue wetting his top lip.

"I told you, no."

He looked around him nervously, then lowered his voice. "You might want to change your mind when you know what I found."

I glared at him. "What are you talking about?" I never swore in the kitchen. Never gave anyone the impression that I was anything but a timid, quiet girl.

"I was in the store, getting some stuff. I saw your shoulder bag." His eyes gleamed, his mouth twisting. He wiped it with the back of his hand.

"That's none of your business." I was watching the others, but they weren't taking any notice and mercifully couldn't hear us.

"Couldn't resist a little peep in there. Nice dress. Black. Black tights, too. And stiletto shoes. Very cool. So you sit and watch movies at night? Nah. That's bollocks, Joanie. You're a fucking Goth! Out on the town."

"It's none of your business."

"Don't worry. My lips are sealed. Your secret is safe with me." He sniggered, like a fucking schoolboy.

I just glared at him.

"Nothing to be ashamed of. Kind of kinky. I'd like to see you dressed up in that stuff. Very sexy, I'll bet."

"In your dreams," I said quietly.

"Yeah, wet ones, Joanie."

"You vile –"

"I can do Goth, too. Or punk, if you like."

"Why can't you just get the message?"

"You want me to fuck off, right. Okay, I'll do it. But if I do, I'll make sure the others know about your little secret. I'll show them your stuff. Shit – can you imagine what Chef will make of it? He'll probably do his nut. Hell, he might even sack you. Don't want no fucking Goth contaminating his food, eh?"

"You're a proper little shit, aren't you?" I whispered.

"Ooh! You speak the language, too. Where's the little mouse hiding now?"

I brushed past him and went to the storeroom. My bag wasn't there. The bastard had taken it and hidden it somewhere, probably in the male toilet.

"I'll give it back, and not a word said," he told me, leaning on the door frame, preventing me from going back out into the kitchen. "For a price."

I felt my fists clenching. Jesus, I could so easily have hit him. My job would have been blown, though. I didn't want to lose it. It wouldn't be easy getting another one, and not with a shit reference.

"One date, that's all," said Dez. "And wear that Goth stuff." His expression was lascivious, disgusting. He was already imaging groping for me.

"Give me the bag."

He shook his head. "Oh, no. Date first. My flat. You can change into your stuff when you get there. You know what, Joanie, you might even enjoy it."

I was screwed. As long as he had my bag and the clothes, I wasn't going to be able to wriggle out of this. Christ, I was going to have to go through with it. One date. One night of horror.

"I don't want anyone to know about this. Not the date, the clothes, any of it."

"Right. So we have a deal?"

I made for the door, reluctantly nodding, but he still blocked the way.

"Sure. My silence. Promise. How about one kiss just to seal the deal?"

I felt my guts clench. The thought of being kissed by this fucking reptile made me want to puke. He straightened up, about to lean towards me.

Behind him there was a growl. Chef was back. "Hoy! Dez, you suppurating boil on a leper's arse! Get on with your work. Leave the women alone."

Dez was off like a scalded cat.

"He annoying you?" Chef grunted.

I shrugged. "I'm okay, Chef."

"Okay. Start cleaning up. We've got a lot of work on tonight. You started early, so you finish at six, okay?"

I went back to my work and kept my head down. I could feel Dez trying to get my attention, but ignored him.

Eventually, when the worst of the frantic evening's work eased off, Dez slid across to me. "Come back home with me."

"I need to get back to my own flat first. Shower and get ready. I'll come to your place for ten."

"Proper night bird, are you? That's okay. I'll get you a taxi."

91

"No! I'll get a tube."

"Won't be many tubes after ten. You'll have to stay the night. Only got one small bed. Cosy." He made that revolting suggestive face.

"One night," I said. "Then I get my stuff back."

"You might like it. You might want more. It'll be our secret, Joanie. No one will have a clue what's going on. Right under their noses. They'd never believe it."

"What's the address?"

When I got back to my flat, I couldn't wait to get into the shower and scrub myself down, as much to get rid of the stink of the kitchen and its Dez-soiled air. The thought of having to go to his place later made me sick with disgust. But he had my clothes. He'd split on me.

I dressed in the plainest clothes I had, old jeans, sweatshirt, baggy jacket, flat, scuffed shoes. No make-up. As un-sexy as I could make myself, which wasn't hard. I'm no oil painting. I slumped on the settee. The previous night and the day's work caught up with me and I dozed off. More than that, I slept.

Those huge crow-things were waiting for me. I tried to claw myself awake as they encircled me in the darkness, scavengers, hungry for something, like they wanted me to give them something – me, I guessed. One opened its beak, blood dripping from it on a long, gleaming thread, inches from my face. I wrenched my head aside and found myself looking into the face of another of the creatures, sitting beside me on the settee. Only this one had a human face. The face of the guy I'd slept with the previous night.

He opened his bloodshot eyes and nodded. I felt the cold dribble of blood from the thing above me and burst awake. The air trembled in the aftermath of my scream.

I looked at my watch. I had an hour to get to Dez's

place. I splashed cold water on my face, grabbed a small bag and left. Outside it was a shit night, drizzling and murky, but that was okay. I didn't want anyone to see me. I pulled the neck of the jacket up and hunched forward, head down. There were a few teenagers on the streets, kicking a ball about, swearing. I got a few catcalls, but they didn't bother me, not after the things in the dream and their terrible hunger. Keep going, don't stop.

The tube was quiet. I found a lonely carriage. Couple of people, like me, inconspicuous. No eye contact. Fine. Gradually the carriage filled up, but as the bodies pressed I became even more anonymous. A couple of older women loomed over me, yattering to each other, never looking down at me. Fine.

I got off the tube and merged with the thick flow. Up at street level, people split up, thinning out. I crossed the road, a horn blaring at me, but I kept my hands in my pockets and danced away. The drizzle was coming down thicker, almost a mist. I was just a blur. I felt the cold touch of the rain on my face and remembered the cold drip of blood in my dream. I shuddered.

I had a twenty-minute walk, through some side streets and then into a rough area to the housing estate where Dez had his flat. I had to step over more than one sprawled body. Drunks and the homeless. Some curled up in sheets of newspaper or brown cardboard, although the constant rain had soaked these makeshift houses. People shrunk into their tiny, womb-worlds. Bottles filled one alley, clanking as I tripped through them. In one place there was a fire burning in an oil drum, with a few figures huddled round it. I saw their faces briefly, the desperate eyes, the last spark of humanity.

They were too dishevelled and down-beaten to stop me, like soldiers after a disastrous battle, crushed by defeat. Not even enough energy to spare me a glance.

I saw the flats ahead. Rubbish and twisted railings stretched out on either side of me. Like this place had never been clean. Fucking massive rubbish tip. Most of the streetlights had their bulbs smashed, lampposts bent over and twisted. Like a war zone. It had its own fetid smell, a rich, noxious stench.

I wound my way up a stair, following Dez's instructions. His flat materialized on one of the landings, its door chipped and wasting, graffiti daubed over it, swastikas and all the usual filth the thugs liked to spray. I almost felt sorry for Dez, living in a shithole like this, but then I pictured his leering face. He was a creep. Fuck him.

As I knocked, something shifted along the landing in the shadows, a hunched figure, obscured by rain and night. I could smell urine and vomit. The figure was dragging itself toward me. Dez opened the door and I barged past him into the confined tunnel that was a short hallway. I heard the door slam and Dez slipping a couple of bolts.

"You made it. Good," he said, smiling thinly as if he didn't know what the fuck to do now that I was here. All talk. Probably never had a screw in his life. A few sick gropes. His hands were shaking. I just nodded.

"Where are my clothes?"

"You want a coffee or anything?"

"No, I want my fucking clothes."

He was too nervous to argue. "Go through," he said, opening a door into his living room. It wasn't the big tip I'd expected. So he'd made an effort. Big deal. Settee, single chair, electric fire, one bar on to warm the place. Clammy air, almost as bad as the kitchen we worked in. The TV was on, some crime show, guns going off, explosions. No surprise.

"I'll get your stuff." He disappeared while I stood, waiting. There were a few books on a shelf, comics and magazines, and a pile of CDs and DVDs. I wasn't interested in looking through them. Sleaze, for sure.

He came back in with my bag and held it out to me. Now that it came to it, he was a bit nervous, hesitant. I snatched the bag. He stiffened. My attitude had made him braver. Tried to put on his usual tough act.

"There's the bedroom. Go and change," he said. He was standing by the door to the hallway, making sure I couldn't make a run for it. I'd never get the front door unbolted in time to evade him if I did get past. I went into the bedroom and shut the door, waiting to see if the creep would try and follow. He didn't.

I opened the bag and pulled out my crumpled Goth gear, clothes, necklace, bangles and shoes and dropped them on the narrow bed. The bag should have been empty, but there was something in the bottom. Another bag, a plastic carrier, a supermarket bag. What the fuck? I got it out slowly. It was double wrapped, two plastic bags. Something soft and wet was inside.

This was some kind of sick joke. Dez being a complete shit. What had he put in here, and why? Trying to fucking scare me, make me more vulnerable? I unwrapped the first bag and held the sides up to the light. Shit, there was blood in there. I opened the door and went back to the living room.

Dez was pacing up and down. He swung round, disappointed to see me still in my ordinary clothes.

"What the fuck is this?" I said, holding the bags out to him.

He flinched, looking at the plastic bags. "I dunno. What is it? Where d'you get it?"

"You put this fucking mess in my bag."

"No. I just saw your clothes and shoes. Was that in there? What is it?"

"You're a fucking liar." I tossed the bags to him and his hands came up instinctively and caught them. He was frowning now. Nice attempt at deceit. He opened the first bag and saw the mess inside.

"What the –?" He started to open the inner bag and must have seen the contents. His face went white, as if he was going to puke. "I didn't do this –"

He looked so shocked I almost believed him. "That's blood. Stuff from the kitchen? That where you got it?"

"No, no. I never."

I went over to him and snatched the bags from him, rolling them up.

"What are you going to do?" He was shaking, frightened.

"You want me to stay the night, I'll stay the night. But if you put one fucking finger on me, I'll smear this mess all over you. You want to be a Goth, or a punk, or a fucking Hell's Angel, then you'll *be* one."

His mouth sagged and I knew I had him. He wasn't going to try it on me, not now. Whatever the fuck this stuff was, however it had got into my bag, it had done me a favour. I thought he was going to piss himself.

"You take the settee," I said. "And I'll have the bed. And *this*," I added, holding up the plastic bags, "will be under my pillow."

"You're fucking mad. A lunatic."

"You're a sicko." I could feel something had uncoiled inside me, my anger and disgust at Dez, everything boiling up after weeks of his unwanted attention in the kitchen, writhing into life, demonic maybe. Fuck, it felt good. Horrible, but so good. I wanted to make the bastard squirm. I should have gone home –

there was still time to get a tube back to my place. No, I was going to make this a night to remember for him. Afterwards he'd never bother me again.

He slumped down on the settee. "You can go," he said feebly.

"Too late for that. You stay there. I'll go when I'm ready. Just don't try coming in the bedroom."

He nodded and I went back to the bedroom and shut the door. There was a small bathroom off the room and I used it to clean up. When I got on to the bed, I slid the plastic bags under the pillow to one side. I stayed dressed and pulled the single duvet over me. There was a lamp beside the bed and I left it on. For a long time I looked at the ceiling. Dez didn't make a sound in the living room.

I must have dropped off to sleep, because the next thing I was dreaming. Not nice dreams, either. They rarely were. Dark things coming at me, prodding, groping. Always heading the same way, towards that nightmare darkness, where the huge crow-things gathered. They loomed, dripping, hands like talons, stretching out, *wanting*. The terror they stirred up was worse than ever. I couldn't stand it. It was leading to something horrible, something I couldn't face. I'd go mad.

I woke screaming, but the sound was choked, as if I'd left it in the dream. Had Dez heard me? I looked at my watch. Gone 3 AM. Maybe he was asleep. I waited. Nothing. No noises from next door.

I slid off the bed. No way was I going back to sleep. Not with those things waiting for me. I couldn't do it alone, though. I'd fall asleep, I knew I would. Those things would drag me in and finish what they'd started. Fuck knew what they were going to drag me into, but next time they'd do it. I needed help.

97

Dez. It had to be him.

I looked for my Goth gear. It was on the floor at the foot of the bed. I picked it all up, the skimpy black dress, silver necklace and the rest. I changed. There was a small mirror in the bathroom. I checked myself over in it. The clothes were crumpled, the tights had at least one long ladder. I'd do. Dez wouldn't be able to resist.

I opened the living room door and peered out. Dez, like me, had slept with a lamp on. He was snoring. I couldn't bring myself to touch him. I picked up a small cushion from one of the chairs and tossed it at him. He jerked awake, staring around him dumbly.

"Dez," I called.

He swung round and saw me, standing there in my tight Goth dress and stilettos. He swore, swinging his legs off the settee.

"Is this what you wanted to see?" I said softly.

"Fuck me," he said, his breathing loud in the half light. Horny boy.

*

I got to the restaurant in the early hours, knowing that Jackson, the caretaker, would have opened the back door and started his daily chores, down in the basement. When he saw me at the foot of the stone steps, he nodded.

"Morning Miss Joanie," he said. He was always polite, to all of us. He must have been in his eighties, looking after this building and a few others in the block for years. It kept him going, gave him a purpose. Other than that, he kept to himself and never asked any questions.

"I've got some stuff for the furnace," I said. "We've got a busy day, lots of orders."

"That's good for business," he said, his speckled face a moon in the shadows.

"Chef wants some of the rubbish cleared away now. Don't want to wait for the refuse men tomorrow."

Jackson was used to us kitchen workers bringing stuff down to be incinerated, as long as we didn't lug sack loads down there. He was from another age, when health and safety didn't rule everyone.

"What you got?" He went to the main furnace, a huge, fat boiler, and used a metal rod to pull open its narrow door. White heat blazed inside.

I held out the double-wrapped plastic bags I'd brought back from Dez's flat. "Meat," I said. "Can't use it now. Gone off. Chef says to get rid of it."

"Chuck it on, then." He stood aside and watched me as I tossed a double-wrapped bag into the furnace. There was a brief whoosh of sound as the intense heat flared.

"All done?" said Jackson, wiping sweat from his face.

"One more," I said. I had my hessian bag with me. In it was my Goth gear. That and another plastic bag, squeezed down into the bottom. It was leaking, but the clothes had absorbed most of the spillage.

"Shame to throw away a nice bag," said Jackson, squinting at it.

"It's out of date."

"You kids! Out of date? In my day, if you had a decent bag like that, it'd last you for years." He laughed.

"I've spoiled it. Some eggs got broken inside." I tossed it into the fire before he could say anything else.

He shut the door.

"Thanks," I said and went back upstairs. The others were arriving.

An hour later, Dez hadn't turned up.

"Where's super-dick today?" said Chef irritably.

Super-dick? I thought. No. Not at all. I picked up my knife and started on the fish, neatly slicing and filleting. I'm very good.

THE BOY ON THE TRAIN

Paul Lewis

Even though it was Sunday the train was standing room only. Wayne was glad he had got on at Paddington or he'd have had no chance of finding a seat. Given how much he'd put away over the last few days, that would have made a long journey even more of a pain. Now his back ached from a cheap hotel bed and his mouth tasted sour from too much beer. With the benefit of hindsight, Wayne decided those farewell pints with the lads before he had caught the train home had not been such a great idea after all.

By Bristol, the crowded carriage had thinned out, freeing up seats for those standing in the aisles to claim. Wayne's head lolled against the window as he tried to doze away an incipient hangover, only for an abrupt pressure in his ears to snap him awake when the train entered the coffin darkness of the Severn Tunnel.

That was when he saw her. She was in an outside seat across the aisle and slightly further along the carriage from him. She was facing his way. From her anxious expression, the way she chewed her lip and fussed with her hair, she seemed almost desperate to be somewhere else.

Maybe she'd been out on the razz too and the constant hubbub of voices and the relentless rocking of the train was having the same nauseating effect on her as it was on him.

He found himself staring at her. Not that she was

any kind of looker. Could have been anywhere from thirty to fifty. Her face may once have been pretty but now appeared haggard, lined with worry, her blonde hair tied back tightly, exaggerating the tautness of her features. He'd seen the look before, if not the woman. The housing estate he lived in was full of them.

Briefly he feared she would catch him watching her. But it was soon apparent there was little chance of that, the woman being too preoccupied with whomever she was travelling with to look in his direction. The grotesquely overweight man reading the *Guardian* in the aisle seat next to Wayne prevented him from seeing the woman's companion.

Whatever. None of his business. He rested his head back and closed his eyes, but the motion of the train and the rustling of *Guardian* pages denied him any hope of sleep. He just wanted the next hour, or however long it was, to pass quickly so he could get home. On the other hand, thinking about the inevitable bollocking that awaited him there, he wondered if maybe he should not be too anxious for the journey to be over.

The fat man got off at Newport. Wayne stretched out, relishing the freedom of space. By now there was nothing to see outside but darkness and his own tired reflection. Soon the rocking of the train and the absence of broadsheet rustling left him drifting off. By then he had lost all interest in the woman. Her troubles were exactly that. He had enough of his own.

When she leant over to ask if he minded keeping an eye on her kid he was startled enough to say yes.

He wouldn't have if he'd been properly awake and thinking straight. A man couldn't smile at a child these days without being regarded as a kiddie fiddler. But she must have been desperate if she'd resorted to entrusting hers to a stranger, and a washed-out and dishevelled one at that, and he simply could not bring himself to say no.

"Oh, thank you," she said, with such gushing gratitude it was almost pathetic. Wayne's reservations disappeared. If anything, he felt good about agreeing. Being lumbered with a kid when you needed to do something alone was a scenario he was familiar with.

"No problem," he said, mouth dense with tiredness and alcohol.

"I won't be long. Thank you again. And…"

"Yes?"

"Nothing," she said. "It's just…I'm sorry."

Before Wayne could ask her what she had to be sorry for, she had hurried off along the carriageway, swaying in sympathy with the train's motion, reaching out to steady herself on the headrests as she passed them.

As she went through the sliding door she glanced back with what to him looked suspiciously like pity or maybe sadness, but certainly something other than gratitude.

Odd, he thought. What was even weirder, though, was the sudden realisation that he hadn't yet seen the kid he was supposed to be watching.

When Wayne looked across the aisle, the boy was staring right back at him.

Maybe eight or nine years old, the kind of unremarkable features the eye tended to slide over. Dark hair of average length. Wearing jeans and a shirt that seemed far too flimsy for the March weather. Ordinary would perhaps be the kindest way of describing him. He certainly lacked the kind of fetching looks that made old ladies stop to make a fuss.

Wayne nodded at him. "All right, mate?"

The boy just stared, fixing him with the darkest eyes Wayne had ever seen and which were his sole remarkable feature.

"Your mum asked me to look after you while she's having...um...while she's in the ladies. That okay with you?"

Stupidly, he found he was struggling to make small talk. With a kid, for fuck's sake. Maybe he hadn't sobered up as much as he'd thought. He glanced along the carriage, hoping the woman wouldn't be long returning.

Then he realised the boy had taken the seat next to him.

"Ah, no," Wayne said, lost for words again, worrying about how this might look to anyone else. "Maybe you should go back to your own seat, you know? Just in case anyone takes it before your mum gets back."

The boy said nothing. Just stared up at him, and Wayne could not help but look down to meet his gaze, drowning in the dark depths of his eyes.

"Well, okay then. Not going to do any harm, yeah?"

The boy nodded and when he took hold of Wayne's hand his skin felt both cold and comfortingly warm.

They continued the journey in silence and got off when the train reached Swansea Central. The station was all but empty and the night felt almost shockingly cold after hours of artificial heating. Wayne zipped up his jacket and went out into High Street, the boy still holding his hand. With the last bus having left several hours earlier and the house too far to walk to with a kid in tow, he had no choice but to flag down a taxi he could not really afford.

"Been anywhere nice?" the driver asked as he did a U-turn and set off towards Morriston, looking at Wayne in the rear-view mirror. If he thought it strange for a child to be out after midnight, he gave no sign.

"Twickenham. Went up for the match, stayed the extra night."

"Don't blame you. Beating those bastards is always worth celebrating."

Wayne said nothing about being so pissed he had missed the train after the game and had been obliged to find a cheap hotel, as if forcing the memory from his mind meant he could somehow escape the consequences.

Carole had made her displeasure clear when he had called to explain in a slurring voice. *Baby to look after, didn't have money for him to waste, should have been ashamed of himself, selfish bastard.* On and fucking on, her voice a digital banshee in his ear. First time in years he'd met up with his old college mates for a Twickenham pilgrimage, paying for the ticket and train fare by working overtime so it wouldn't screw up their budget. First time in years, and she had to just go and take the fucking shine off it.

The taxi reached Morriston and headed up to Clase where Wayne got out at St David's Avenue and, a tenner lighter, led the boy up the drive to the front door, adrenalin pumping in readiness for the row he knew was only a few moments away. If he was lucky Carole would have fallen asleep. Unlikely though. Most nights she would doze off in front of the television yet somehow always managed to stay awake if there was a row in the offing.

The front door opened directly into the living room of the housing association semi they'd spent six months on the waiting list for. Sure enough, there she was, standing by the sofa, arms crossed, looking as if she'd been slapped. Clearly, she had rehearsed this moment in her mind all day. "Decided to turn up, you selfish little shit," she started, voice hushed so as not to risk waking the baby, but venomous all the same.

Then she did an almost comical double take when Wayne led the boy inside. For once she appeared genuinely lost for words.

"Oh, yeah," he said, shrugging. "This. I can explain." He couldn't, though, not really, because he didn't understand it at all. Yet whenever he found himself wondering why he had brought the boy home instead of doing the right thing and calling the police, an icy numbness stole through his brain, turning his thoughts to mush.

"Just…just forget it," she said, sighing, and they said no more about it.

The boy released Wayne's hand and went over to the sofa, where he curled up with his eyes closed as if he had gone straight to sleep.

Carole headed upstairs without another word. Wayne followed her but did not go straight to their room. Instead he showered away the sour odour he could smell on himself from wearing the same clothes for two days.

When at last he walked naked into the bedroom it was to find his wife either asleep or pretending to be. She did not stir when he slid into the bed next to her. Within moments he was asleep too, a sleep so deep he barely heard Samantha crying for her feed at some ungodly hour and was only distantly aware of Carole getting up to see to her.

Breakfast was no different to their usual routine, except Wayne had no need to rush. The rugby trip was the starting point, and supposed highlight, of a week off work, so he took his time eating, instead of cramming down toast while rushing to catch the bus over to Morfa and his job as a supermarket supervisor. Since the baby's arrival he had got into the habit of waiting until the last possible moment before leaving for work. Driving would have been easier, but the car was a SORN job, parked up on the driveway because they couldn't afford to get it through its MOT.

Supervisor. Wasn't that a fucking laugh. All his university education had bought him was a few quid an hour over the minimum wage, a salary so pathetic he hadn't had to start paying off his student loan yet.

Carole was remarkably cool given how close they had come to a bust-up last night. Wayne frowned. The expected row had fizzled out for some reason or other, though for the life of him he could not recall what.

The late autumn weather was sunny and pleasantly warm, so they put the baby in her buggy and walked the short distance to Morriston Park. He was momentarily surprised when he felt a small hand suddenly close around his. The boy. Carole looked down at the kid and smiled, then began steering the buggy with one hand so the boy could take hold of the other.

An elderly couple approached, with a dog on an extending lead that resembled a lifeline between them. Wayne vaguely recognised the couple and of course at the sight of the buggy they were compelled to stop so they could coo over Samantha. Suddenly realising there was no sign of the boy, Wayne looked around anxiously, only relaxing when he saw the kid darting behind a tree. Presumably he was playing some made-up game. If so, he won because the old couple never once mentioned him.

Later, back home, they sat in front of the telly, talking about what to do tomorrow if the weather stayed fine. Making plans on a budget pretty much summed up their shitty lifestyle and before it was time to make dinner they'd agreed to get the bus into Mumbles for a walk along the promenade. Fare aside, they'd only have to pay for couple of bags of chips. Not exactly the Costa Brava but it was cheap. Literally as cheap as chips.

It would have been funny if it hadn't been so fucking sad.

Wayne was aware of the boy watching them intently, taking in every word of the conversation but contributing nothing. Anyone would have sworn he wasn't a part of the family. Kids, Wayne thought, shaking his head with bemusement.

He slept badly that night, his dreams filled with images from the last few days jumbled together in haphazard fashion. A woman he had never seen before yet who looked oddly familiar was shouting at him, her eyes wide either with anger or fear. Her shouts turned into a baby's shrill crying before morphing into screams that halted so abruptly he could hear their echoes as he suddenly jerked awake. No, he thought, with a sickening lurch in his stomach. Not echoes of screams. Someone was screaming. It sounded like Carole.

Instinctively he turned to reach out for her, but the other side of the bed was empty.

The screaming did not so much stop as fade into a slow and horrible gurgling. A whirlwind of scenarios, all of them terrifying, played out in his head as he leapt up and charged out into the landing and across to the baby's room. The door was partly closed, and he shouldered it open.

For a moment, his brain made no sense of what the pale light through the curtains revealed. The pastel yellow wall behind the cot appeared to have been randomly sprayed with darker paint. Backing away from the sight of it, he reached out and turned on the light.

"Oh no," he whispered. "Oh, Jesus *Christ* no."

Carole was sprawled on her back on the floor alongside the cot, arms outstretched, eyes open wide but seeing nothing. Her throat had been slashed, the wound a wide red smile, and her nightie was stained black with blood from that and the multiple wounds in her chest. The wall nearest to her was splattered with it too, like some demented artist's canvas.

Even if shock hadn't rendered him immobile he could tell at a glance there was nothing he could have done for her. Nobody lost that much blood and survived.

Moaning quietly, trying desperately to deny the undeniable, he forced himself to look across to the cot. And cried out in utter despair when he saw what was inside.

The door creaked softly as it closed behind him.

A headline leapt into his head. *Burglary gone wrong.* He'd read it so many times, tabloid jargon for something that was only supposed to happen to other people, but which was the only explanation his jellied brain could contrive.

Wayne turned around. There was no intruder. There was only the boy.

He had taken a knife from the kitchen. Its blade was coated with blood that dripped onto the floor as he held it out.

Put the knife down, Wayne wanted to say but speech had been denied him.

He dropped the knife anyway.

Feeling as if he was struggling through water, Wayne bent down to pick it up, driven by an irresistible compulsion to touch it, to know for sure that it was real and that he wasn't just having some fucking awful nightmare.

His hand closed around the handle, long enough to confirm it was real, then let it go.

He knew he should call the police but all he could think of was getting out, to put as much distance as possible between him and them. Not out of the house, just out of that room, somewhere that meant he would no longer have to look at what had been done to his wife and child. Only then did he become aware he was naked. Somehow it felt wrong, almost obscene, so he went into the bedroom where he grabbed some clothes and, having dressed, ran downstairs with the intention of calling 999.

Instead, though, he searched for and found the car keys, and went outside. Though he had neither planned nor wanted to do it, he felt like something outside of his own thoughts had taken control of his actions.

It was not quite dawn. The road was deserted. Nothing stirred. The windows of the house adjoining theirs were dark; the previous tenant had been kicked out for dealing and the association had yet to reassign it, which in the circumstances was probably for the best.

Further along the avenue, the shutters were down on the Spar and the newsagent next to it. Were it not for the lights of the DVLA tower, that great squat block that loomed over the estate like some giant alien ship, the place would have felt utterly lifeless.

Wayne got into the Focus, which turned over and turned over twice more before starting, its reluctance due to it having been parked up for six weeks. Only as he drove off did he notice the boy in the passenger seat. Wayne couldn't remember him getting in.

With nowhere to go he drove aimlessly, crossing from one side of the city to the other and back again. There was so little traffic at this early hour he only had to stop for red lights. Despite his trembling hands, the havoc in his guts and the grief and pain that speared him, that threatened to reduce him to a quivering wreck, he was careful to stick to the speed limit, not wanting to risk being stopped. He was in enough trouble as it was.

After all, his prints would be on the knife handle.

By the time the first signs of congestion appeared with the onset of rush hour he was cruising along the seafront road, a mile or so outside the city centre. There was no reason to believe the bodies had been found yet. Probably wouldn't be for several more hours, maybe longer. Carole's mother had an annoying tendency to show up uninvited whenever she felt like, but of course she would not suspect that her daughter and granddaughter's ravaged bodies were slowly cooling in the nursery. She'd just assume they had gone out.

Still, he couldn't risk it. His mother-in-law had a key to the house to keep an eye on it during the infrequent occasions he and Carole scraped enough cash together to spend a few days in some ancient caravan in Trecco Bay. It would be just his luck for her to decide to take a sneaky look round on the assumption the place was empty.

The police could be looking for him within hours. They'd get his car registration and it was surely only a matter of time before they found him.

On impulse, he turned off into St Helen's Road and went across the city to High Street, where he left the car in a one-hour bay. He didn't lock it. No point. He was never coming back. For the same reason he didn't think twice about going to the station and using his credit card to buy a ticket to London.

Most of the carriages were almost full already but he found a seat towards the back of the train and sat with his head down, bending and folding the ticket in his hand and tapping his feet on the floor, a nervous twitch he was powerless to control. When the train pulled away, so smoothly at first that it seemed as if it was the world outside that was in motion, he felt himself slump. There was no going back now, in more ways than one.

Keeping his eyes on the window even when they stopped at a succession of stations meant he wouldn't have to look at the boy, who had taken the seat next to his. Whenever he tried to think back to the scene in the nursery, a dense mist filled his head. Likewise, when he tried to go over the events leading up to it, mainly why he had brought the kid home at all.

They stopped at Cardiff and again at Newport, where he felt the boy take his hand and the heartache and guilt that threatened to cripple him washed away. Now he understood with perfect clarity what he had to do to make things right. There was a middle-aged woman in the seat across the aisle from him, travelling alone. She was gazing out the window too, and for a moment Wayne felt he could see inside her soul. Whatever had happened to her to make her life such a misery remained unknown to him.

Nevertheless, it was enough to mark her.

"Excuse me," he said.

She looked up at him with an uncertain half-smile.

"Yes?"

"Would you mind just keeping an eye on my kid for a couple of minutes? I need to use the gents."

"Not at all," she said, though he sensed reluctance in her tone.

"Great. Thanks so much." He turned to walk away, then the mist in his head cleared enough for him to understand the consequences of what he was doing, the fate he was condemning her to. Too late now, he thought, for apologies.

He went through the sliding doors, along the next carriage to the vestibule beyond, where he stood by one of the exit doors with the window down. He knew exactly where they were now. Moments before the train hit the Severn Tunnel, he leant as far out of the window as he could and closed his eyes before the darkness rushed in to take him.

DOUBLE EXPOSURE
Jonathan Mitchell

I rented the room because it was cheap. I didn't know anything about Crawford Street or the old house.

I had a furnished upstairs room with slanting walls and an old-fashioned kitchenette. Mrs. Neely, the landlady, had given me permission to store some things in the attic; that seemed as good a place as any to tuck my paintings away. Why didn't I just throw them out? I certainly didn't hang onto them because they made me happy: in seven years I hadn't managed to sell a single one. But painting had been the only creative distinction in my life, and I couldn't totally reject my work even if everyone else had. So I kept them. On the evening of the day I moved in, with a flashlight in my hand and the canvases under my arm, I opened the attic door and peered into the gloom.

There were cardboard boxes of various sizes, stained with splotches of dried squirrel dung, and a few piles of books. A torn lampshade sat forlornly in one corner. I trudged to the opposite end of the attic and propped my canvases against the wall, the painted surfaces facing away from me so the squirrels couldn't get to them. As I turned back, the flashlight's beam fell on a panel nailed to the bottom of the adjoining wall. It was discoloured, and the nail heads were orange-brown with rust. I thought it over for a minute or two, went back to my room and got a hammer.

Returning to the attic, I squatted down in front of the panel and shone the flashlight on it again. It had obviously been in place for a long time. What was I going

115

to find? Probably nothing interesting, but I was curious and there wasn't much else to do. With the claw end of the hammer I pried out the nails, and there was a little creak as I pulled the board away from the wall.

Strange as it sounds, I wasn't surprised when the flashlight revealed a bundle of paintings. In fact, I laughed—it seemed absurdly appropriate. I reached through the crudely cut opening in the wall and eased the canvases out. They were bound with twine, and a sheaf of papers—yellow with age and folded in half—had been tucked under the knot. I carried them to my room.

The papers were evaluation sheets for an art correspondence course that had been completed in May 1970. The painter, someone named Reed Kessler, had failed the course and it wasn't hard to see why: if my paintings were mediocre, his were terrible. A still life with a bowl of ugly, misshapen fruit, a landscape with warped trees...the instructors at the Llewellyn School of Art and Design in Cambridge, Massachusetts had tried to be diplomatic, but there weren't many nice things to say. Still, the painting at   the bottom of the pile was interesting. For Reed Kessler it must have been a heroic effort. The canvas showed a young woman with dark blonde hair sitting under a gazebo; wearing a sleeveless white dress, she looked directly at the viewer and smiled. It was not a masterpiece, but it had a certain intriguing quality. My gaze kept returning to the woman's face. There was no evaluation sheet to go with this painting, so it must have been something that Kessler had painted for his own pleasure. If the instructors had seen this final canvas, they might not have flunked him.

It was getting late. I made a sandwich, watched TV for a little while and went to bed.

*

The next morning, I started awake when I heard my cell phone ringing on the nightstand. It was Andy from work, asking where I was. I craned my neck to look at the digital clock, which read 9:17. Dammit! How could I have forgotten to set the alarm? I thanked Andy for calling and hurried down the hall to take a shower.

A few days later, I sat at my landlady's kitchen table as she made coffee. I was interested enough in the canvases I'd found in the attic to ask Mrs. Neely about the tenant who had painted them.

"Well, Mr. Warren," she said in carefully genteel tones, offering me a large mug with steam coiling from the top, "I'm older than I care to admit, but that was before my time—before my husband acquired the property, anyhow. We never had a tenant named Reed Kessler, and I can't tell you the first thing about who the tenants were forty-eight years ago. Except—"

"Yes?"

"Well, every so often someone complains about having a funny feeling in that house. Upstairs tenants, in particular. We got the place in 1981 and the previous landlord used to hear the same sort of complaints: cold chills, the sensation that there was another person in the room when there wasn't."

I swallowed bitter coffee and tried to smile. "So it's haunted?"

"Isn't every old house haunted?" Mrs. Neely shrugged. "Anyway, it's just a funny little thing that some people notice and others don't. I hope I haven't rattled you! Is your coffee all right?"

"It's good," I said, risking another sip. "Thank you, Mrs. Neely."

I went to the library, where I leafed through a local phone book: no listing for Reed Kessler. Then I signed in to use the Internet for an hour. The Social Security Death Index showed me two Reed Kesslers, one of whom had died locally. Born October 23, 1942; died June 14, 1970. That wasn't much more than a month after he'd failed the painting correspondence course, and I felt eerily certain that Kessler had taken his own life.

I checked my e-mail, deleted a lot of junk and returned to my room on Crawford Street. There was nothing to do that long, quiet afternoon except stare into the strange eyes of the woman Reed Kessler had painted forty-eight years earlier. Who was she? Had he painted her in this room? Had he *died* in this room? The woman didn't answer: she just looked back at me with burning eyes, a little smile pushing up the corners of her mouth.

The next evening, when work was over, I walked out to the parking lot with Andy. "Hey," he said, "I'm going to meet Lori down at The Hideaway for a couple of drinks. Why don't you come along?"

"Nah, I'm beat. I think I'll just head home. Thanks, though."

Andy's brow furrowed. "Tom, you're doing okay, right?"

"Yeah, sure. Why?"

"I don't know. You just seem a little down lately. I can't remember the last time we went out for drinks or anything else."

It wouldn't have done me any good to deny what he was saying, so I didn't. I just tried not to dwell on it. "I, uh, haven't been sleeping well. Something to do with the new place I'm renting, maybe. I'm sure I'll settle in eventually."

Andy's worried expression made it obvious that my response hadn't satisfied him. "Well, anytime you want to hang out or get a bite to eat, just say the word. Lori would like to see you again, too."

I winced inwardly. Lori didn't like me at all, but Andy was my friend so he was reaching out. "We'll get together soon," I said. "You guys have a good night. I'll see you tomorrow."

"See you then, man. Get some rest."

*

I heard the voice for the first time that night. It was low, not much louder than a whisper. I couldn't understand what it was saying; I only knew that it was a man's voice. It spoke steadily for a few minutes and then, abruptly, was gone. I didn't know what to make of it. When I got tired I went to bed.

At some point I dreamt of summer light, fuzzy and unreal as if seen through gauze. Gradually, a gazebo became visible among trees with lush green leaves. I approached it and saw a human figure sitting in heavy shadow. I squinted, peering into the gazebo, but the face remained indistinct. Jerking awake, I realized that I had been dreaming: the room was still dark and the digital clock read 3:39. I checked to be sure that the alarm was set and went back to sleep.

*

It became harder to get up for work each morning. More and more often I would show up at the office with stubble and a wrinkled shirt. At the end of the day I'd grab a burger from some drive-thru and rush back to my room.

Every two or three nights I would hear the voice. Some of the things it said were becoming intelligible, and I began to look forward to these "visitations".

I wondered if any of Reed Kessler's relatives were still living in town. Consulting the phone book at the library again, I wrote down three numbers and addresses. One of them was in an old subdivision called Pinewood. That had the right ring somehow, and one Saturday afternoon I drove there.

The tree-lined streets were unnaturally quiet, the gently sloping lawns empty of children. An air of desolation hung over the faintly shabby, single-story ranch houses. Finally I rolled to a stop in front of 136 West Pinewood Drive. I would have to call each number to be sure, of course, but even then I knew I had the right house. It was a small red brick home with wrought-iron railings, and there was absolutely nothing remarkable about it. Someone named Gordon Kessler lived there. I was about to take my foot off the brake when I looked between 136 and the neighbouring house at a patch of grass heavily shaded by trees. For a second, maybe two, I thought I saw something else there: a gazebo, the kind a lot of people used to have if their backyards were big enough to accommodate them. I felt dizzy and squeezed my eyes shut. When I opened them, the gazebo was gone.

I forced myself to take several slow, deep breaths before looking again: still no gazebo. (Naturally! It had never been there in the first place.) I gave the car a little gas, eased down to the stop sign at the end of the block and drove back home.

*

The following Saturday, I called Gordon Kessler. Yes,

Reed had been his younger brother. The voice in my room on Crawford Street had nudged me, imparting a strange certainty even when I couldn't understand what it was saying. Gordon Kessler asked me to drop by, and to bring the painting I had spoken about.

I drove into the subdivision, moving along West Pinewood Drive. Ahead of me the street dipped downward, then rose again and wound its way between more lonely-looking houses and tall, skeletal pines. Without warning I felt myself gripped by a searing flash of need, as if I were experiencing some other person's hunger: the desperate hope that things would be—*must* be—better over the next hill. As brief as it was painfully distinct, the sensation had passed by the time I pulled into the driveway of the red brick house.

Mild-mannered to the point of shyness, Gordon Kessler was in his early seventies, with a bulbous nose and a bad squint in both eyes. He seemed pleased, if a little bewildered, that someone wanted to talk to him about his brother. I sat on his sofa while he sank into an easy chair and examined the oddly compelling painting of the woman. "Reed did this? I've never seen it before."

"Yes," I answered. "It was in a bundle of paintings he left in the attic of the Crawford Street house."

"Crawford Street," he murmured, propping the canvas against the right side of his chair with an old man's careful movements. "That's where he hung himself, you know."

"Well, I knew that he had died, but I wasn't sure how. After I'd found his paintings and the documents from the correspondence school, I did a little checking around at the library." I paused. "I'm sorry. This can't be easy to talk about."

"Reed and I grew up here. When my father passed

away and we moved my mother into a nursing home, it just seemed natural to come back. Now my wife is gone, too, and I never see the kids—so there's only me." He shrugged.

"Did Reed always like to paint?"

"It was something he picked up in college, and he kept at it till the end. Reed had a tough time. He drifted from one thing to another, but he worked very hard on his paintings. That's why it hurt so much to see him fail. But this one," he said, pointing a gnarled thumb in the direction of the canvas, "this one is *inspired*."

"I feel the same way. I wish the people at the correspondence school had seen it."

"Yeah. So his paintings had been up in the attic all this time, huh? Damnedest thing." He smiled again, shaking his head. "Forty-eight years! Well, this is definitely one of Reed's, what with the gazebo and all."

"You recognize it?" I asked.

"The gazebo? Oh, sure. It belonged to the Hearns, our next-door neighbours. Good Lord, that thing was torn down so many years ago. It fascinated Reed; he would sit in the backyard and stare at it when he was a kid."

My spine prickled. "Do you know who the model was? Did the Hearns have a daughter?"

"Three sons, no daughter," Gordon Kessler said gently but flatly. He drummed his fingers on his knees. "Reed would ask people to model for him, but they always said no. I doubt that this woman ever existed outside my brother's imagination. He made her look awfully real, though!"

I nodded, getting up to leave. "Mr. Kessler, would you like to keep the painting?"

"Well, that's very nice, but why don't you hang onto it? You're the one who found it, after all. Maybe you were meant to have it."

I thanked him and left with the canvas. Funny, but I still didn't know what Reed Kessler looked like. Probably he had shared Gordon's bulbous nose and permanent squint, suffering all the limitations those features would have imposed. But there had been something extraordinary about Reed Kessler, and he had transferred it into the blazing eyes and unaccountable smile of the woman in the painting: the woman who had never been real. I took her back to Crawford Street, the bleak ranch houses of Pinewood receding in my rear-view mirror.

I guess I was a little disappointed at first. The full weight of old Gordon Kessler's remark—that the woman had existed only in his brother's imagination—didn't strike me until a few days later. After work I was sprawled on the bed, smoking, when suddenly I realized what the painting had embodied for its creator. I knew what it *was*. I got up, stubbed out my cigarette and looked at the canvas: it seemed now to have acquired more subtle detail, to have been painted by a more skilful hand. I thought of the flash of longing I'd had in Pinewood and saw that the woman's cheeks had become infused with colour; I thought of hunger and desperation and saw that her eyes didn't just smoulder but were bottomless pools of scalding dark water.

No, the voice that drifted in and out of my room on Crawford Street had not misled me. I understood.

*

I didn't hear the voice anymore after that. I didn't miss it, really, because it was just one aspect of a presence that continued to surround me, a presence in which I luxuriated. Time began to lose its meaning, and I stopped answering my cell phone. A few days ago there were urgent footsteps on the stairs followed by an insistent, almost angry knock at my door. It was Andy, the final thread connecting me with a world to which I had never belonged in any legitimate sense. He tried, he really did, but by that time I hadn't gone to work in days and they didn't want me back. (That's okay. My rent is paid up for the month and I have everything I need: the room, for the short time that I will continue to occupy it physically, and the painting.) I stood on the landing, watching Andy go, and I haven't left the room since then.

Occasionally I drink a little water. The lights are off in the daytime, and at night I stretch out on my right side and turn on the nightstand lamp so that I can contemplate the painting. It is made of hunger, and as the days grow shorter and I grow weaker, the painting becomes more and more beautiful. "Isn't every old house haunted?" asked my landlady, and at times I do sense earlier, fainter presences still attached to the boxes in the attic, the mouldering books and the torn lampshade. Layers of hauntings, generations of ghosts? Why not? Maybe this house is the final stop for lost souls: maybe we're drawn here so that what has been broken all our lives can finally be mended. Or maybe Reed Kessler just encountered an obstacle on the road to the paradise he had imagined, and painted, for himself.

The slanting walls seem to have fallen away. A constant wind blows deliciously cool and I feel something like the change of seasons, the movement of enormous gears. The painting is no longer a painting but a window, and the woman is emerging from the gazebo into the blazing light. Her smile is ravenous, the look in her eyes beyond description. She extends her hand and I reach out to take it.

My brother Gord—I mean, Reed Kessler's brother

Gordon—said that maybe I was supposed to have the painting. I think he was right. And I think that, this time, I'm here to stay...

NIGHT FLIGHT
Eric Ian Steele

It was only when the old man's gnarled fingers stopped twitching and hung from the lacquered arms of his rocking chair like mottled claws that we both started running.

When we came to the bus stop we bent double and started to laugh. We hadn't been running long, just a couple of blocks, but it seemed like forever. We breathed in sharp air that stung our lungs like marathon runners, feeling the surge of anticipation and relief that comes with leaving.

We would have to go now, there was no question. We had discussed it often in those long hours of early morning that had spun out into too many weeks, talking in low voices in the stuffy little room by the light of a naked bulb. It had seemed unreal then, a thing that could never happen. Now it had happened, and the unreality of our situation spread out before me like a road map to nowhere and anywhere.

We stood upright, and there was a moment of silence as we face each other – an instant of uncertainty. The future, so ominous, so massive. So many questions lacking answers.

No-one would follow, I was sure of that. We had done our job too thoroughly, planned it too meticulously to admit any detail, any flaw.

So we had run, hand in hand, as fast as we could, not out of desperation, but out of exhilaration. We laughed without a reason to laugh. The bus stop brought us to a halt, where we came under the owlish stare of an old woman with a trolley.

We must have seemed strange. Cherry, barely eighteen, three years younger than I was, both shimmering with summery sweat, breathing loudly, shaking with exertion. Grime encrusted her clothes. My shirt sleeve was ripped where his hand had been. She wore jeans ripped across the knees, not from any fashion but because she only had that one pair. She wore one of my old sorts because her Aran sweater till hung from her bedroom door.

It had come upon us all of a sudden.

An old man at the end of the queue turned to look at us. He had a pinched face, thin cheeks, and eyes surrounded by crab-coloured meat behind his wire-rimmed spectacles. His eyeballs seemed fixed in his skull by only the thinnest folds of grey flesh beneath his bony forehead. His head was raised off the pavement by a long, greasy brown raincoat that hung from his shoulders like curtains. I imagined them opening wide to the sound of a movie-theatre organ to reveal a sagging skeleton filled with raw, red offal like rotted fruit.

I dropped his gaze and looked beyond him as if expecting a bus that was approaching. There was none. The old man took a drooping cigarette from his lips and tossed it to the ground, not bothering to stamp it out. It lay there, giving off a faint, orange glow and wisps of smoke, making a pathetic plea for someone to extinguish its life, alone there on the street.

I resisted the urge and glanced into a dimly-reflective shop window, half-lit by narrow tubes of neon. I studied the faces of the people in the queue in that reflection, a line of shadows. Anything to avoid looking at Cherry. Anything to avoid the hell of talking.

I came to my own face in the reflection. All that was visible were areas of blank nothingness cast by the shadows of my eye sockets, nose and jawline. My hair, usually flattened to my scalp, was pulled out of shape where he had tugged at it, growing out of the side of my head in an unruly jungle, my face some dark planet. I puckered and spit into my hand, pressing down the mess just as the bus arrived. I was glad it had. I didn't want to look at my reflection anymore.

The vehicle shuddered to a halt with a mechanical shriek. The door opened with a hiss. I sought in my pockets for some change and realized I had left all my money in my jacket pocket which was, of course, in the apartment.

I turned to Cherry and told her, expecting a rebuke. Instead she held out her hand. It contained a pile of loose change.

"Here, take it. It's enough."

"Where did you get this?"

"It was his. I don't want it. Take it."

We sat down together on the back seat of the bus and collapsed into the welded chrome and leather. The fluorescents over the aisle cast pale, uncomforting light that brought out the hard edges of her nose and chin. Her shirt rippled in the breeze from the open slit of a window. I pulled it open wider and felt the cooling touch on the slab of my forehead. I closed my eyes and laid my head back.

From under my lids I could see the sun dive below the tallest building in front of us, charring their outlines into blackened skeletons against its burnt hugeness. Gold spun across the blue sky, lapping against purple candy-floss clouds as the first stars peeped out under cover of twilight. Above, a ghost moon rose, a phantom stone, spectral, smiling.

I felt a weight press into my chest and the scent of dusty attic windows and lavender potpourri. Cherry placed her head below my shoulder, holding the other with her hand pushing herself into me. She looked up to see if I would say anything, went to kiss my chin, then she reconsidered and dove her free hand between my legs, caressing my groin.

Like a fool, I asked, "Did you do that for him?"

She withdrew her hand, leaned away from me and turned toward the window.

"I don't want to talk about it."

She was looking at the doors now. They seemed to be a football field's length away, yet still I felt uncomfortable.

I had no idea what she was thinking, I realized with a stab of panic. I had done so much for someone I knew so slightly. But it was too late to go back. She held all the cards. If she left me now I'd be on my own again, alone. And she could talk. If they found her she could tell them everything.

Dark thoughts entered my head and I shook them away physically.

"We talked about it often enough," I said.

"That was before. It's done now." She turned to stare at me. There was anger in her face. But anything was better that her looking at those doors. And what she said was true. Maybe I'd hoped it would stay a crazy dream. But, as they say, everything changes.

Everything had changed.

I changed the subject. "Do you think they'll find us?"

"No," she said. No hesitation. And why would there be? We had torched the place, hadn't we? "And even if they did," she added, "do you think they'd care?"

"I guess not," I said.

Maybe she's right, I thought. Maybe they would suspect his own daughter had done him in. But maybe not.

And either why they would have no evidence. None. We had been very careful about that. The stove left turned on, the frying pan doused in oil, the curtains set alight. We had backed out with the whole place on fire. All that would be left was a blackened skeleton.

"Do you want me?" she asked. There was a smile on her face, but it was a mere mask. There was something desperate underneath it.

"I love you," I said. Of course, I did. Why else would I have done it?

"Yes, but do you want me?"

I looked around to see if anyone was watching, then wrapped my arm around her, a heavy, dead thing that felt like a diseased log. She grinned, and I knew she was enjoying pretending to be small and fragile in my embrace.

She was difficult to hold, and I lowered my head as gently as I could into her short, tangled hair, a choppy auburn sea. She wasn't really pretty. Not move-star looks. She had no place on a cinema screen, only on the street outside. A waifish look, perhaps. But maybe that was just my romantic sensibilities. Her skin was pale and I could see the soft, downy hair on her cheek. Her eyelids were dark without make-up, something gothic and disturbing that I liked about her.

I rested my head against the metal rim of the seat. My mind ached. I hadn't slept for two nights, thinking that perhaps if I deprived myself of rest there would be no last-minute pangs of conscience. As it turned out, there were none. In fact, if I'm one hundred percent honest, I enjoyed it. Something bestial lurks within each of us, I suppose.

My brain felt on fire. My temples throbbed. My eyes pulsed with blood, making my vision blur. Or perhaps I was making my vision blur on purpose.

"What are you thinking about?" she asked.

"You know what," I said without looking.

"Was it worth it?"

I found myself wondering the same thing. "Yes," I said.

"It felt right at the time, didn't it?" she asked. "But now, I don't know. It feels like everything's catching up with us."

"Do you wish we hadn't done it?"

This was a conversation I had dreamed about. The words were almost the exact ones which I had rehearsed in my own mind days before. Was I dreaming? The unreality of it all hit me again. I had to turn and look at her to make sure I wasn't asleep.

She was staring back at me, eyes wide, face taut, close to breaking.

"No," she said. "But can we face it all?"

"All what?" I wanted to break away from her gaze. I couldn't bear it. "There's nothing for them to go on, you said it yourself. So they have the folders we sent, so what? Do you know how many people get away with what we've done? Lots."

Her eyes quivered. She wasn't smiling any more. It was her turn to panic.

"But what if they do?"

"They won't. We just disappear into the sunset. That's all."

"Maybe we could go back and explain," she said. "Maybe they wouldn't do anything if they knew."

I stared at her. *Don't you want this?* I thought. *Don't you like being free? Is it too big for you?*

She crossed her arms and stared out the window again. She was sinking into one of her moods. At first, they had only made her seem lovelier. Now they frightened me. She could do anything, say anything. Where would that leave me? I told myself she just needed a period of time to adjust. I told myself that without her moods she would become predictable, and that without unpredictability she would become tiresome.

I almost believed it, but my heart was racing too fast.

I told myself to calm down.

Suddenly she grabbed me again, pulling me close. Her eyes were sparkling, her grin sharp and vulpine. "It's all right," she said. "I'm just being silly. It'll be okay. Won't it?"

I nodded. Of course it would. We were together and we were free.

Have you ever had a memory that's both pleasant and difficult to recall? It's like that with him. I don't want to remember, and yet I do.

When I close my eyes I can see him, can feel my fingers sink into the thick, quivering folds of flesh that hang loosely from his jowls like the flesh of a withered pig. He looks up at me with those hateful, wax-dummy eyes, eyes brimming with watery tears not of pain or pity but of anger and contempt. He reaches up for me with those clammy, liver-spotted claws of his, hissing through false teeth that have become dislocated from his gums in the struggle and jut out from his palate.

He was in the living room. The sun outside was dying, sending out waves of gold in its death throes across the sky. The molten fire baptised me through the windows. Sitting in his rocking chair, watching TV, it was easy to sneak up behind him, to put my hands around his wattled throat and... squeeze.

He tried to shout for help, but my fingers had already crushed his larynx. My fingers are strong, good for grasping. I'd been practising, using the power grip strengtheners they sold in the sports shop. As I pressed tighter his face turned crimson, then purple, then his lips turned blue. I'd nearly lost him when I felt his hands grab me, one last fit of strength from this dying old vulture. He tore my shirt and clawed my face. I thought he was going to get lucky and take out an eye.

Then Cherry was there, sitting astride his legs, holding him down with all the force she could muster, gabbing his arms, smiling up at me. The same lupine gleam in her eyes. It was fearsome how much an old man could struggle. He clung to life like an old leech, just like he had clung to her. But against two people he had no chance.

She sat there on his thrashing legs, pinning his arms to the chair, grinning up at me as I squeezed his throat so hard blood came out where my nails dug in. I felt - actually felt - the last puffs of his breath pass through my hands. I felt his windpipe buckle and collapse. Rain washed down my face. I looked out the window at the sky and I saw that it wasn't raining and of course we were indoors anyway. It was the tears coursing down my face.

In the end his head flopped to one side like a rotten beetroot, and his lungs emptied with a stale, hollow sigh. His eyes turned to salt and poured out onto his lap.

But we only started running when his fingers stopped twitching.

The bus continued onwards. Nameless streets flashed past, dusk fading to twilight and then to darkness and night.

Cherry turned to face me, and there was a strange glint in her eyes, a kind of sparkle. "I know where we're going," she said. "But where are we going to?"

I said nothing. I could only listen to the steady whisper of traffic in the lanes ahead, to the dark surf of blackness that lapped around us all on the bus, and could only stare at the dim, red headlights swimming in that darkness like aimless shoals of fish, mad or lost. The silence was as intimate as a soft kiss or her embrace.

The bus, meanwhile, moved on.

THE LONELY PASSION OF JIMMY TATE
Trevor Kennedy

'He who fights with monsters might take care, lest he thereby becomes a monster. And if you gaze for too long into an abyss, the abyss also gazes into you.'
(Friedrich Nietzsche, German philosopher, 1844 - 1900)

I was just twenty years old when I first took the DTs. It happened during a holiday with a group of friends in Majorca, Spain. I had been drinking heavily for several days and in my youthful innocence had initially thought it to be a severe case of sunstroke. Little did I know at the time this would become a regular feature of a life plagued by alcoholism and addiction. This is the story of the very last time I took the DTs, and the day I died.

Part 1: DELIRIUM TREMENS

I awoke suddenly from disturbing lucid dreams of sinking in quicksand and choking with thirst. According to my old, battered mobile phone it was 11:03pm. I knew it was around that time anyway, by looking outside my open window on what was a calm summer's evening, which was darkening quickly in the moonless sky above. It would be pitch dark very soon. I couldn't really remember falling asleep, but I had a feeling it was sometime in the late afternoon. I had slept on the sofa again, in my small, ground floor bedsit flat, the floor of which was now a vast swamp of alcohol and tobacco-related empties. Empties which included, but were not limited to; numerous beer cans, three empty litre vodka bottles, empty cigarette packs, a half-eaten Chinese meal now covered in ash and cigarette butts, crisp packets, a dirty ashtray, and several bottles of cheap cider, also containing the aforementioned butts and ash. Cigarette ash was everywhere. It was as if I had upset the gods in some terrible way and they had made it rain ash all over my humble little abode as punishment. My physical appearance at the time wasn't much better either. I was unshaven, unwashed, with greasy hair and skin. I had also apparently lost some weight. My attire at the time consisted of a pair of old white shorts and a red t-shirt which was covered in what looked like cider stains and cigarette burns. It had rained ash on me also. I looked and felt like shit. But first things first. I made the quick dash to the kitchen sink in the next room beside the living area, where I ran the cold-water tap, put my head underneath it and drank until my great choking thirst and dehydration were temporarily relieved. The flat around me felt desolate and cold; I was beginning to feel deep anxiety, mixed with loneliness and fear. I had been in this situation countless times before, but its familiarity did not make it any easier or more tolerable. I couldn't help but think that someone was watching me from outside the sitting room window, observing me from a secret and hidden place, somewhere in the grassy playing field and trees that peered into my personal circus sideshow of self-detoxing shame.

As I lay back down on the sofa, my thoughts turned to a post-mortem of the last few days: Wetherspoons Bar. Cheap pints. Chatting with girls. Whiskeys. Taxis. Unknown nightclub. A scuffle. Threats from anonymous young men. Phoning friends and family at silly-o-clock. Trips to the off license. Watching old black and white films on DVD. Music on. Roy Orbison. Radiohead. David Bowie. Music too loud. Neighbour above me complaining about the noise. Mess. More mess. Blank. Blank. Blank. Actually, there were lots of blank spaces and missing time. I also now had a throbbing headache and realized that I needed to relieve myself in the toilet immediately, which I proceeded to do in the bathroom beside my front door on the other side of the flat.

I sat on my inglorious throne in the bathroom, knowing I could be doing with some Librium tablets to ease this motherfucker of a hangover, but alas, I knew I didn't have any in the flat, and I would have to wait until the morning to get some from the doctor. This was going to be a long night without them. After briefly considering my predicament, I dismissed the idea of going to the hospital for a proper, professional detox. I decided I would just have to stick it out at home, alone, for at least a few days until I would be fit enough to actually face people and the world again. 'The Fear', as we alcoholics call it, was now kicking in with great gusto. And then it came. It came like a great flowing, luminous yellow river of stink and pain. I leaned over to the bath beside me and violently vomited out the bile from my stomach, which was mixed in with some water, dead cider and lots of little pieces of chicken and chips from my half-eaten Chinese meal. It looked like some sort of disgusting radioactive soup dish. The pain in my stomach from relieving myself of it was sharp and immense. Once finished, I returned to my makeshift bed on the sofa, wrapped myself in an old beer-stained blanket which was close by, and after some tossing, turning and adjusting I eventually drifted off to sleep again.

Part 2: FOR WHAT YOU DREAM OF

Thick black curtains. Long, thick, black curtains with strange, indecipherable symbols and lettering on them. That was the first thing I remember seeing in the dream. I cannot remember if this is how or where the dream started, but these curtains appeared to be a starting point of sorts, regardless of what may or may not have come before. I didn't like those curtains. They felt wrong and filled me with a dread which made me realize something very terrible and most probably malevolent lay behind them.

And what were these weird, mysterious letters and symbols which emblazoned it? A form of witchcraft? An ancient old language? My sense of dread was now evolving into an eerie anticipation, mixed with a sense of urgency and fear. I did not want to walk through the curtains... but I did so anyway.

The room in which I found myself in next was more of a darkened long corridor. I walked, no, not walked, more like floated, down this eerie passageway. I noticed the walls to each side of me were adorned with vivid old paintings in a classical, ancient and Dante-esque style. Each depicted great battles between angels and demons, grotesque abominations torturing the newly dead souls, decapitating them, ripping out their stomach innards, castrating them and cutting off the penises of their male victims. Other paintings depicted what appeared to be a skeletal, dress-wearing, female grim reaper in a field at night, harvesting new and fresh souls. These images were so graphic that this dream of mine had now entered lucidity; I was consciously aware that I was dreaming. However, I got the impression that I was trapped in this dream state, unable to awaken from its vivid terror.

When I reached the end of the corridor, I noticed more of the strange black curtains in front of me. I floated through them.

The room I now found myself in was much more substantial in size, although it was entirely darkened and had no windows. There didn't appear to be any of the creepy paintings there either. In front of me, the room seemed to stretch out as far as the eye could see. My surroundings now looked slightly familiar. It felt like I was in an old factory shop floor, though there was no machinery or workforce to be seen. Perhaps I had been here before in my waking life? I suddenly felt that I was being watched and even followed by someone or something, and this made me feel intensely anxious, full of an overwhelming dread.

As I floated further down the apparent factory floor, the being behind me appeared to be catching up with me, almost literally breathing down the back of my neck. I was too frightened to turn around and confront my, as yet, silent and unseen stalker, and even if I had wanted to, I don't think the mechanics of the dream would have allowed me to anyway. All around me I was now beginning to hear the faint cries and distant screams of someone, somewhere ahead of me. My phantom companion was still directly behind me, its foul-smelling breath filling the air all around. I quickened my pace and moved on down the dark factory. As the horrible screams and wails intensified and became more loud and closer-sounding, I eventually found myself in what appeared to be a new room or part of the factory. To my left, I could see a naked man who looked a little like myself, strapped to a metal chair, where he was screaming, pleading and begging for mercy from his apparent torturer, who stood over him, directly facing his victim. This humanoid torturer appeared to be some sort of demon, though headless, and with two legs and feet which resembled those of a horse. Neither of the two seemed to notice or become aware of my presence. I was merely a spectator in all of this, though I still felt that my phantom was standing directly behind me. The man screamed in agony and terror as his headless torturer carved something onto his chest with the huge, sharp knife he was carrying. The chest carvings appeared to be more of the weird, indecipherable symbols which I had noticed earlier on the black curtains. Where was I anyway? Was this Hell, or at very least my own personal vision of Hell? I felt a fear which I had not felt in a long, long time come over me, freezing me in terror, unable to move, with my skin crawling, and the phantom lurking somewhere close behind me, the stench of his foul breath all around.

Suddenly, I noticed a glimmer of light appearing on the far-right wall of the factory. I made my way towards it as quickly as was physically possible within the strangely different laws of physics which governed this dream hell of mine. As I got closer to it, the gleam of light became more visible and abundant, until it manifested itself into what appeared to be a transparent, glassless window and possible escape route into a brightly lit - and apparently daytime - outside world. I rushed towards it as fast as the dream would let me, my phantom pursuer hot on my tail, my heart beating faster and faster. When I finally made it to the window, I jumped through it with all my might into the bright daylight world in front of me...

And then I woke up.

Part 3: THROUGH A MIRROR, DARKLY

I woke with a panicked jump. The blanket which was wrapped around me was now soaking wet with sweat. My body, forehead, and hair were also covered in a cold moisture. I looked at my mobile phone - 1:26am. The dream had felt very real and essential to me and was now etched firmly into my mind. A familiar nauseous feeling came over me again, and I knew exactly what was coming next. I grabbed one of the many empty off license bags from the dirty floor in front of me and vomited into it, more of the ghastly bright yellow and green bile from deep within my stomach. It hurt. It hurt the back of my throat and stomach like a fucker, but I had to get some of this alcohol-related poison out of me in some sort of way from some kind of bodily orifice.

When I had finished spewing out what felt like my entire insides and guts, I sat back and caught my breath again. A great thirst once more came upon me, so I got up and made the short journey into the kitchen and grabbed a clean pint glass - which I had probably stolen from a bar in a drunken stupor at some point - from the cupboard. I ran the cold water tap until it was almost freezing, filled the glass and quickly knocked back the contents, temporarily feeling slightly refreshed. I now felt hungry too, but I knew there was no way I would be able to swallow, let alone keep down anything in my shrunken stomach for quite some time. I filled the glass up again for later and clambered back into the living room area.

As soon as I opened the living room door, I was greeted by a new, most unpleasant sight. All across the great mess of empties and cigarette-related dirt, was what appeared to be a living, moving carpet of crawling things. Maggots, spiders, flies, cockroaches, and beetle-like creatures were everywhere, so much so that the cream carpet below was no longer visible and there were so many of these disgusting little creeping bastards that they were climbing and scrambling over each other in apparent desperation. Black frog-like monstrosities then appeared to be hopping all over them. On top of them, black and green snakes were crawling the walls. Although I was startled at first, disturbed by this awful sight, when I closed my eyes I realized exactly what was happening; I had been in a situation like this before. My DTs had progressed into hallucinations, and I was now undoubtedly delirious. *No big deal...* I thought to myself... *they are not real. This too shall pass.*

After what seemed like a very long time, but in reality was only a couple of minutes, I opened my eyes and just as I had reckoned, and hoped for, I was relieved to find that the carpet and walls were now free of any moving, crawling or slithering insectoid or reptilian creatures. I lay down on the sofa again and tried to pull myself together a bit more and relax, if that was at all possible.

I still had 'The Fear'.

BANG! A loud noise from outside. I jumped up with a jolt and looked out of the window, into the darkened playing field and trees that resided at the back of my flat. The moonless sky did not help my visibility, and I could not see anything that may or may not have caused this sudden noise. Perhaps it was caused by a dog or cat, or even a late-night reveller making his or her way home from a night on the tiles? It was quite loud though. Just as I was about to turn and sit back down again, I noticed something out of the corner of my eye. In the trees to the left, there was a crouching, pale-faced, apparently male character waving over at me in a childlike manner.

Although I could not make out the person's face properly at first, they appeared to be smiling, or at least grinning, at me through a set of dark sunken eyes. Startled, I did the first thing that came to mind and waved gently back at him, feeling a little silly, though curious. He stood up and waved and smiled at me again, revealing that he was wearing a red t-shirt and light grey shorts. He beckoned for me to come out to him. Worried, confused and with an insidious fear rising up in me, I shook my head in a negative response to this strange figure with his odd gestures. Continuing to smile, as if in a morbid knowledge I was not privy to, he began moving from out of the trees and across the field. He continued towards the locked back door in the kitchen beside the living area where I was looking out at him, watching his strange body movements as he came closer to the back door. It was as if he was hopping or dancing disjointedly towards the door, beckoning me to come to greet him and apparently let him in.

I was now numb and trembling. What the fuck was going on? Who was this strange, creepy guy? He reached the door. BANG, BANG, BANG on the back-door window. Silence. I stood still. BANG, BANG, BANG again. Another pause. BANGGGG!!! Suddenly, and whether it was a case of temporary bravado or just pure instinct and adrenaline, I quickly walked into the kitchen and opened the door to my unexpected guest who had up to this point been pressing his horrid face against the glass and peering in at me nightmarishly. Although he had stepped back into the darkness a little, I could still make out his pale corpse-like features and face. A face that looked familiar to me... almost too familiar.

"What is it? Who the fuck are you, scaring the shit out of me at this time of night?" I snapped at him.

A pause.

"Hello, Jimmy..." he spoke with a knowing smile. "I've come for you. I've come to take you with me, away to a place where there is no more pain and where all your worries and struggles are over."

And then it hit me. Of course, this strange fellow looked familiar, with the old red t-shirt and white shorts. He was me. I was looking at a mirror-image of myself and talking to this doppelganger of sorts. I was confused at first, but I soon felt calm all over, with a tingling sensation of pins and needles rushing over my body. The pain struck next, before I collapsed in a heap on the ground. The last few things I remember, just before I died, were pains in my chest, pains in my left arm, pains in my jaw and neck, feeling sick, being sick, an overwhelming sense of anxiety, coughing, wheezing, and finally drifting off and over to the other side...

I was found a few hours later, on the same morning, by a middle-aged woman out walking her dog in the fields and surrounding area outside the back of my flat. How come it always seems to be those people out walking their dogs or joggers that find the dead bodies anyway? Death by heart attack was the coroner's verdict. There was a good turn-out at my funeral as well. All of my old mates and family showed up, which made me feel kind of loved and popular in the end. Caroline Dobson also made an appearance, and she was in a terrible state, weeping and moping around, and making a terrible fuss about it all. Perhaps she really did love me after all? They even played my favourite song at the crematorium. They say us alcoholics and addicts are haunted by ourselves and our pasts. Maybe this happened literally to me? And the paradox of my existence now is that I have become a ghost, a ghost who will go on to haunt himself in his own past? Who really knows?

Who knows what lies ahead for me now?

THE DOOMED EMPIRE
Andrew Darlington

The tide is retreating across a beach that has no end, trapping lagoons between breakwaters, interlinked by wide deltas shimmering down to meet the pulse of waves. The boy in the navy-blue swimming trunks crouches down to watch. There's a lake of still saltwater seen low across ripples of wet sand, across formations of weed-slimed stones and stranded crab-crawled pools. An inland sea, fed at its highest point by a system of tributaries, broached at its lowest point by a narrow outflow spreading towards the far sea-line.

Between those two upper streams would be the city, for there must be a city. This will be the place where wandering nomadic tribes first gather in uneasy alliance, where the rivers meet and dilute into the greater body of sea. Hastily erecting defensive earthworks against the wide continent beyond and chewing out harbour-mouths along the waterfront for small fishing-boats to skitter beneath wheeling gulls.

It was there, concealed by fine drifts of wet sand, that he dug out the human skull.

It is 1956, a week's summer holiday in a lozenge-shaped off-white caravan in Cowden. The sky drizzled relentlessly for the first two days. At one end of the unsurfaced lane is the 'Cross Keys' pub where the buses from Hull pause, on their way up the coast towards Hornsea. A little way along the lane's spur there's a small store flanking the campsite entrance, with magazine-displays and spiral-stands of postcards. There are scattered standpipes across the muddy field, where campers can fill containers with water for washing and cooking.

At the lane's farthest terminal point, paced along the thistle-grown cliff-top, there are abandoned houses teetering on the eroding brink of imminent collapse. Tiptoeing inside through disappeared doors appropriated for kindling, over buckling boards, they smell of urine and decay, wallpaper and plaster hangs from the walls like rind. A few forlorn rags and pathetic limbs of broken furniture glisten damply. Every inch of lead or copper piping thieved, power and light-wiring fixtures and fittings extracted from conduits. Sometimes the rooms echo with the mournful phantoms of former residents. But today when he shouts through the door-space, his voice simply echoes.

The North Sea laps in drab silver, as if it's an organism breathing in sleep. Its breaklets of liquid ice explode up between his toes and wash across his feet. He glances back at the inland sea. Glimpsing images shivering in the slight breeze, ghosts in the air catching at the corner of his eye. Whispers that defy all logic, shimmering fables and fancies embroidered by loose pieces of imagination, hints of mythology, slivers from some other reality leaking across dimensional interfaces, only partially there.

His bare feet go slap-slap-slap on wet sand. He'd toyed with naming the city Roosley, but that doesn't sound true. Perhaps it's pronounced Rh'Slie...? But he decides on Faraway instead. It exists before history. Between ice ages, as glaciation recedes, leaving meltwater lakes and lost seas that drain away southwards. He'd done sketches in the caravan's pale calor-gas light. The city walls form a ridged half-circle. First mounds of earth, then reinforced by timber palisades with regularly spaced watchtowers. Finally there are cyclopean ramparts constructed of dry-stone blocks, with parapets and guardhouses, the main gates forming a giant open-mouthed skull. A walled community of shabby hovels, market stalls and makeshift palaces tracked by winding alleys that smell of sweat, wood-smoke and open middens. It becomes Babylon, Rome, Byzantium, overlaid with Atlantis, prehistoric comic-book 'Conan' cities, and HP Lovecraft geometry.

He has a small plastic boat, a tug constructed in two sections. The upper part is faded red, the keel and underside is white. It stands in for the first fishers who leave the river-mouth and venture into the sea in skiffs, hugging the shoreline, never daring to go out of sight of land. Putting into natural bays and coves every now and then they encounter other, less settled tribes, to barter and trade. When there's a misunderstanding and two of the fishers are killed, Faraway dispatches a punitive force, annexing the insurgents, extending its zone of iron influence along the northern seaward rim.

Clearing a channel, his hands dig deep into the pool of clear water, penetrating the event horizon of another lucid world where tiny darting fish flit through their liquid element, and shells form small gaping mouths. Stubbing against hardness, his fingers wriggle down into the sand around a stubborn obstruction, staining the water in swirls. Easing and forcing the object this way and that until it sucks with a drowning gurgle. And he dislodges it up, slowly, dripping and dribbling. A smooth off-white surface roundness. Two empty sockets. He lifts the skull until it's level with his face, squinting eye to eyehole. Its touch burns like electricity, in a sharp migraine memory-hail seen through nearly closed lids.

Set back a step or several from the cliff-edge there's a low domed café resembling an amputated Nissen hut, where – if your Mam buys a mug of tea and you get a Vimto, you can perch on the bench outside and eat your own food. He dislikes the effervescent nasal burp-back of the fizzy drink, but Mam made strawberry-jam sandwiches, carefully wrapped into greaseproof paper. She made them this morning, so the jam's had time to soak up into the slices, making them rich with sweetness, but also more rigid than bread is supposed to be. His mother reads about romance and treachery in her magazine, as he hears the soporific sound of the radio crooning from inside the café. The music, a soft sleepy droning reassurance that nothing can ever disturb this world's calm ever again, is carried on the crisp golden aroma of chips. Mam says the café man smokes a skinny cigarette, drooping ash in an unhygienic way. Best to eat the sandwich. Wriggling impatiently, he can feel the splintery bench roughness on his bare legs, as jam trickles on his chin.

He's bored. There's a crude pathway, spaded out from the dirt, reinforced by rows of wooden pegs, zigzagging its way from the cliff-top down to the beach. He's already eager for the beach again, its dryness shelving away in honey-peppery granules, across acres of wetness, to the surf.

Faraway is extending inland, its growth attracting migrants bringing in raw new cultural mixes. While voyagers in triremes with painted sails navigate further, mapping the tides on epic voyages, skirting realms of sea-serpents and barbaric pirates down to the far southern shore, establishing two colonies on either side of the outflow channel. Noting with concern how the torrent of their sea empties over the edge of the world, draining away into nothingness. Yet this is Faraway's thousand-year golden age of peace and prosperity under the enlightened rule of the elected Council of Ten.

Across different lives, he is a farmer. A carpenter who works his hand in wood. He's a baker. He sells fruit from a stall in the souk, weighing the scales with lead. He's a mariner crouched at the gunwale watching the unwinking amber jewels of shore-lights set into the stiff grey ghosts of the city, lost across the distance of mist-speckled air. He's a soldier in bronze armour, trudging south beneath the hot sun, his crested helmet carved into the jaws of a sabre-toothed tiger. His comrades have helms shaped to resemble bears, or scorpions, savage wolf-fangs, sea-monsters or mythic beasts. And Faraway endures.

The tide is retreating across a beach that has no end, dreaming beneath its shroud of light. The breakwater stippled with barnacles. The boy in the navy-blue swimming trunks crouches down, sinking onto one knee within the enclosed pool of trapped water. He lies carefully down full length, the indentation of his limbs stirring smoky eddies, tensing against the cold, until his body is submerged. He sinks the lower part of his head into the water, until he can look across the pent-up lagoon from its own perspective. Seeing ghosts in the air that shiver at the corner of his eye.

He can see out through the skull eyeholes, through the last mist of sentience lurking within that cave of bone. See dark city fortifications and enclosing harbour arms behind which ships strain restlessly at their mooring tethers. Fragments of imagination spin loose, slivers from some other-dimensional reality. Loosening the glue that holds time together. If he allows himself to slip further, to sink down into the depths of the inland sea in a nightmare of terror, eyes wide as ripples break over his last desperate gasp, arms flailing as swirling currents grip his limbs, the undertow will carry him deeper beyond hope of rescue. The current is swift, unrelenting, he'd tumble, borne out to sea with no chance of reaching dry land again. Will he surface elsewhere, to be washed up onto the if-world of the Faraway beach? Can he sit in sun-warmed shallows and watch the triremes scull out across the sea-lanes towards the colony-towns sited along the southern shore? Hear the plash of oars, the shouts of mariners.

Turning right, and walking along the cliff-top in that direction, there's a former World War II army exercise zone with square concrete bunkers and a shooting range, wired off for use by territorial's for weekend war-games. Some of the local children who live in static caravans, sneak in under the wire ignoring the Ministry of Defence warning-signs, and scour up a collection of spent cartridge cases from the weed-covered mounds. One boy lines his shiny prizes up on the path, a row of half a dozen, like hazardous skittles.

Turn left along the cliff-top in the other direction, the winding path twists its way beside a copse of trees. His mother holds one finger to her lips secretively and warns "don't succumb to the heebie-jeebies and the foggy and frosty hobgoblins in the woods awaiting," hurrying mock-rapidly in mile-eating strides on towards the next village. "Where are we going?" he whispers, in case the beasties overhear. "There and back, to see how far it is." His mother carries a shopping bag. Inside the bag, carefully wrapped up in pages from *The Daily Mirror*, is the skull he'd found on the beach. There's a church in Mappleton. And a Police House. They will know what to do.

Yet already the pool is shallower than before. As the

tide recedes, the trapped waters escape. The two northern feeders reduce to a trickle. Ribs of sandbars appear. There's panic in the city, and an exodus of migrants south. Following a coup an emperor seizes emergency control with strict martial powers. He commands the construction of a barricade across the outflow channels, to staunch time. There are grumbles of dissent among the vigorous energetic colonies.

The boy in the navy-blue swimming trunks drags a large stone into the centre of the outflow stream, places smaller stones to either side, then banks sand up between them to form the barrier. The dam succeeds. He stands back and watches with some satisfaction. Until the torrent bursts free further along, unleashing a tidal wave across the wet sand. The colonies rebel, declaring their independence. Faraway is darkening. An aging organism increasingly bitter and corrupt, shrivelling in on itself. There are naval battles, lit by arcing comets of Greek Fire, incandescent bursts burning up the sea where screaming men howl curses at vengeful gods. Followed by a simmering stalemate, as Faraway retracts inwards, and dies. Fallen parapets, cracked pinnacles of collapsed masonry. All the while, the lungs of the sea breathe in soft ripples.

In the Mappleton Police House his mother lifts the package wrapped in newspaper and lays it on the desktop, folds the paper away to produce the skull. The policeman observes it from various angles, pokes it with his ballpoint pen, then summons the vicar, who also happens to be a member of the local historical society. "You'll have noticed that Mappleton has a church, while Cowden does not," he explains. "Yet Cowden once had a church. Over the years the tide has gradually eroded the coastline, taking more and more, year by year, across decades. It took the churchyard first, then the church itself. Some people of a fanciful nature claim they hear the phantom tolling of the submerged steeple-bells ringing beneath the waves." He laughs politely at his own joke. "For a long time graves were exposed along the cliffs, depositing skeletal remains along the beach. My belief is that this medieval skull originated in this way. So no need to call Miss Marples quite yet."

In his head, the boy is protesting, "No, it's older. This skull is much older than that." But he says nothing.

"Thank you for your generosity in donating this item. It'll make an intriguing addition to our modest Library display cabinet. You did well young man, we're very grateful. I'm sorry, but although there's no reward, you're welcome to refreshments while you're here. We have cherry scones?" The vicar's dark trousers are shiny at the knee.

The boy feels cheated, sulky. The holiday is drawing to a close. The prospect of the return home, and school, looms ever closer. The scone and glass of milk are good. The policeman seems grateful to be relieved of the need for the further due process of the law. And the vicar is telling Mam amusing anecdotes about his parish work. Is he flirting with her? By the way she's laughing she obviously enjoys his attentions

A large and hazy sun seeps through veils of cloud as though someone's smearing their bloody fingers across the horizon, yet still dazzling his eyes. On the beach the blood-red tide has receded to its farthest point. The inland sea drained. Faraway is gone, reduced to some shapeless mounds of sand, its standing skull gate a portal from nowhere to nowhere. Even the isolated colonies on the dry southern coast have been abandoned. People drift away, returning to wandering nomadic tribes in a long forgetting. The interglacial draws to a close. The ice returns. Faraway is erased from knowing, gone millennia before the dawn of history. But for a fleeting wraith of empathic memory spilling from the last skull. In the display cabinet. In the Mappleton Library.

REAL LIFE
Franklin Marsh

"You are one sick fuck."

The man picked up the hedge trimmer and advanced on the girl. She was tied to a Black & Decker Workmate, and in a state of undress. The dual blade of the trimmer whirred ever louder. She screamed piercingly.

"How can you watch this shit, Perky?"

Sean took a drag on his joint and turned to his companion.

Perky (Simon Perkins to his parents and workmates) seethed inwardly. He'd been waiting quite a while to watch *The Milton Keynes Ripper*. And now that doped up twerp Sean was going to ruin it. He thumbed STOP on the DVD remote control.

The blood-soaked hedge trimmer disappeared.

"Aw!" moaned Sean.

"I thought you said it was shit," growled Perky, through gritted teeth.

"You're too sensitive," smirked Sean. "You're messing yourself up, just sitting here watching horror comics. You want to get out more. Get yourself a good shagging. Get pissed. Stoned. Have some fun."

Perky retrieved the disc from the machine, pressed it into its case, and ambled toward his Horror Cupboard. He opened the door and surveyed the shelves of DVDs, books, magazines and the odd video. The MKR (as they called it on the internet) went into the Ms. He closed the door and sighed deeply.

"Come on, mate," said Sean, in a conciliatory tone. "Come down the pub with us tonight. I could fix you up."

"No," said Perky, turning and heading for the door to the outside, adding a belated, "Thanks," as he reached it. "Not tonight."

"Wait up!" he heard Sean call, as he walked out into the corridor and headed for the stairs. He increased his pace as he trotted downward. A short jog down the hall, and he burst through the flats' front door into a weak sunshine.

As he walked slowly towards the town centre, Perky reflected on how much he hated his flatmate. Then decided he didn't, because, difficult as it was to admit, Sean was right.

He was becoming a hermit. Holed up in that dingy flat, watching and reading horror. Imagining slicing up people who had offended him in the most trivial way.

As he neared the shops, the concentration of human beings increased, as did Perky's nervousness. He dodged down a short, narrow cobbled alleyway, and then descended a much wider flight of stairs. Another short pathway flanked by bushy shrubs and he found himself on the canal towpath.

Blimey! He hadn't been down here since he was a kid. A dangerous place then. How many boys had ended up in there because of the Milltown Gang? Too many.

Perky ambled a few yards to a grey-painted bench and sat down. Perk up, Perky! That bastard gym teacher. How they'd laughed. He found himself reddening with the memory, and quickly glanced around to make sure no-one was watching.

Not a soul about, apart from a young mother approaching him from the left. Something odd about her.

She was pushing a very old-fashioned pram. A perambulator. Not a buggy. Must be a family heirloom, or a car boot sale bargain.

Perky tried to watch her without being seen to. She was wearing a long black coat buttoned up to the neck. Funny. It was quite a warm evening.

Perky looked around him. Black canal. Grey sky. Grey towpath. Dust covered the shrubs and reduced their greenness. Grey bench. He was clad in a grey zip-up jacket, a white t-shirt, black jeans and white trainers. Two landlocked grey pigeons circled him on the lookout for crumbs, their red legs and feet introducing a tiny splash of colour. A duck slowly navigated the canal, looking straight ahead. Perky supposed it was brown, a female, but the light contrived to turn its plumage grey. A black and white cat watched its progress from a grey wall.

It's a monochrome world thought Perky, and plunged his head into his hands, feeling depressed. What could he do? Continue to drift through life? Could he change? If only something would.

"Perky?"

He looked up in shock. The young woman in the black coat with the pram stood beside his bench.

"It is you, isn't it?"

Her puffy face, a plaster crossing the nose, seemed vaguely familiar, like the corkscrew hair. He frowned. She smiled sadly.

"Don't remember me, do you?"

"Erm..."

"Karen. Karen Sm... Thomas."

"Karen!"

Perky beamed, and his mind rolled backward. Kaz had been the female version of him. Both slightly obese, shy, acned. No netball team for her, any more than he could reach the football first XI.

Average students. Not popular, but not hated. Someone once suggested they'd make a good couple and they had purposely avoided one another for the rest of the year.

"How are you?" Perky said, too loudly.

Karen sat down beside him on the bench.

"I'm married."

Perky's fixed grin remained in place. He desperately searched for a cliche.

"Who's the lucky fella?"

"Carl Smith."

She looked away.

Perky's grin faded. Stuck in clichéland, his blood turned to ice. Carl Smith was your worst nightmare.

The school bully. The classroom cheat. First to smoke, drink, take drugs, and have sex. He said. But if you valued your teeth, you wouldn't disagree. First to leave school... to take up residence in a Young Offenders Institution.

The sort of kid who'd walk down the street and punch someone in the face for the hell of it. Rumoured to have slashed Susan Farris' pony because she'd turned him down at the Prom. There's was nothing he wouldn't do, or force others to. The leader of the Milltown Gang. The other yobs, if you met them on their own, were reasonable. You could talk to them. They didn't live to hurt. Not Carl.

"How did I end up with him?"

Perky realised that Karen had spoken.

"Yeah?"

"I was travelling back on the train from Uni. He got on and recognised me. He'd just got out of prison or something. He seemed so worldly. And he was polite. And charming. He seduced me in First Class. I'd never even been out with a boy. I became obsessed with him. My parents gave up on me. I fell pregnant. I thought he'd never want to see me again, or tell me to get rid of it. But he didn't! He said we had to get married, and we'd get a house. Which we did. Council. But it was a house. After a few months of what seemed like bliss he started to go out without me. And bring people home. Dreadful people."

Karen faltered, and seemed to be trying not to cry. Perky felt helpless and useless. She regained a form of composure.

"I had the baby. He calmed down. But recently it started again. He's taken up with some sixteen-year-old slut. They taunt m-m-m-me…"

She was crying now.

"They do things in front of me."

Karen stood up abruptly and began to unfasten her coat. She turned to Perky and held it open. She was naked underneath. Perky had seen naked female bodies before. In newspapers and magazines. On television and in films. When he realised what was happening he experienced an incredible sexual frisson, until he saw her body. There was a normal human female body under the coat, but it was difficult to make out because of the scars, scabs, cuts, bruises and burns. Perky's erotic charge turned to nausea.

Karen sobbed on and refastened her coat. She turned to the pram and looked at the tiny bundle of clothes within.

"They killed my baby," she whispered.

Perky experienced another shock. He couldn't believe what he was seeing and hearing.

"There must be something you can do," he mumbled, lamely.

Karen reached into the pram and picked up the tiny figure. It somehow didn't look real to Perky. She pressed it against her breast and crooned. Perky sat, frozen.

Karen stepped forward, holding the baby (if that's what it was) at arm's length in front of her.

Perky gasped "No!" as she let go. The baby dropped into the canal with a loud plop. It bobbed up to the surface once, and then slowly sank. Perky was on his feet, watching in horrified fascination as the little pink blob slowly shrank.

Karen's tear-streaked face regarded his.

"Will you go to the police with me?"

Perky so nearly said yes. But the thought of Carl Smith made him hesitate, and then it was too late. Karen turned away with a final sob and stepped off the towpath.

"NO!"

Perky's hand clutched empty air. Unlike her baby, Karen didn't even bob to the surface once. There were just a few bubbles once the initial splash subsided.

Perky gazed down at the now still surface of the canal.

Do something!

What?

Save her! Call the police! An ambulance! Anything!

He looked around. No one in sight. Taking a deep breath, he hopped from the towpath and dropped into the canal. It was bloody freezing! He thrashed around and grabbed the bank. Controlling his breathing he wiped his eyes and prepared to dive back under to try and salvage something.

His feet touched the muddy bottom and he realised that, at that point, the canal only came up to his chin. This gave him courage and, taking a deep breath and squeezing his eyes shut, he submerged once more. Groping blindly, his fingers touched material. He clutched on tightly and drew a large, heavy object toward him. His head broke the surface, and he greedily drew in oxygen.

He pulled the object toward him and coughed with pleasure as he realised it was Karen. So began an awkward struggle to push her limp body back onto the towpath. The waterlogged coat now seemed to weigh a ton and Perky was weakening.

"Come on, Son! Push!"

Perky opened his eyes to see an elderly man in a flat cap, dark blue blazer, white shirt, and paisley cravat attempting to pull Karen up from the land. Her coat rode up and exposed her bottom, and the red lines engraved upon it. Choking on the stinking canal water, Perky managed to pull the coat edge down.

"Well done, lad. You're a bloody 'ero!"

Perky ignored the proffered hand.

"There's a baby in here somewhere," he spluttered, and dived back underwater. He felt the disgusting soft mud of the canal bed squirm through his fingers. As his lungs began to hurt, he touched another piece of material, lost it, then grabbed it again.

Breaking surface once more, he dumped the new burden on the canal side. The old man stepped back and removed his cap. Perky noticed a middle-aged couple with a brace of poodles watching interestedly from a few yards away.

"Call the police! Get an ambulance!" he bellowed at them, as he pulled himself out of the water, and slumped at Karen's side. She coughed. Perky grinned.

Wrapped in a blanket and shivering, Perky sipped at a cup of machine tea, and frowned at the uniformed policeman who occupied the bare room with him. Bare save for three chairs and a table.

The door opened, and a policewoman entered.

"Simon Perkins?"

"That's me."

"Well done, Mr Perkins."

Perky looked away.

"You undoubtedly saved that young woman's life. Do you know her?"

"We were at school together," admitted Perky, grudgingly. "Hadn't seen her for years until today. Coincidence."

He sipped his tea nervously, his thoughts turning to Karen's injuries, and visions of policemen ransacking his horror cupboard and dragging him off screaming.

"Do you know how she came by..."

"...those marks on her body?" finished Perky.

The policewoman leaned forward.

"Her husband, she told me. And his girlfriend."

"Do you know her husband's name?" The tone became harder.

"Carl Smith", said Perky, feeling as though he was signing his own death warrant.

"Ah," said the policewoman, a very grim smile appearing on her lips.

It was after midnight when Perky returned to the flat. Karen hadn't regained consciousness, but the medical staff seemed pleased with her progress, whatever that was. The police took Perky's statement and gave him a lift home. He'd wondered whether to ask for police protection, as the officer in charge had reassured him that

Karen would be taken to a refuge when she recovered, then realised that he'd have to face this alone.

He heard porn-film sounds of ecstasy from Sean's room as he wandered through the darkened apartment to his own tiny quarters. Bastard. He towelled himself down, dragged on shorts and a t-shirt and crawled into bed.

He hadn't drawn the curtains. The moonlight shone on the ceiling, tree branches reaching for him. He heard far away shouts and smashes.

Smith would be coming for him. Of that he had no doubt.

He woke up mid-morning. He tiptoed around the flat before realising Sean wasn't there. He checked the calendar. Saturday. He wouldn't have to 'phone in sick. What to do? Make preparations.

Perky walked down into town and made a few purchases. A hardware shop yielded a carving knife. A sports shop offered up a baseball bat. Passing the junkyard, he quickly grabbed a length of lead piping.

As he headed out of town toward the flats, he saw a tall, gangling, spotty youth loping in front of him. One of the old Milltown lot. Clad in a light-blue shell suit, unlaced Adidas trainers, several kilos of gold chain around wrists and neck, and a fake Burberry cap perched on the very back of his shaven head, the boy turned into a side street.

Perky clutched the lead pipe and left his bag at the entrance.

"Royce!" he shouted, gratified to see the youth start and turn quickly, losing his cap in the process.

"Wot? FukmePerky. Wotchuwont?" The words spilled in a stream from the sneering mouth, which Perky hit dead centre with the pipe.

Royce lay spreadeagled on the ground, clutching at his bleeding mouth. Perky hit one of his knees with the pipe, producing a higher scream.

"Seen Smithy lately?" enquired the assailant.

Royce looked petrified.

"PerkyyamadcuntesgonnakillyamanSharontheykno witwuzyu."

"If you see him again," said Perky calmly, "tell him I'm ready."

The pipe descended on Royce's groin.

Returning home, he stashed the weapons in a corner of the living room and began to rearrange the furniture to form a little square fortress in that corner.

Sean walked in halfway through his defence building.

"What...? Perky? Have you gone...?"

Perky shoved him hard, so that he fell back on the sofa, and felt a spark of elation at the surprise and fear in Sean's eyes.

"Listen, you need to get out. Just for this weekend. Go and shack up with one of your tarts. See you Monday."

"What are you...?"

"Go!" roared Perky.

Sean went. He emerged from his room five minutes later, clutching a sports bag.

"Sort yourself out, Perky, or one of us will have to go," he muttered.

Perky heard the door slam and continued with his work.

He watched the sun set from the flat window. And darkness spread throughout the land, he thought, clutching the lead pipe.

A smile flickered on his lips. Come on then, Smith, he thought. Lord Of The Vampires. King Of The Zombies. Prince Of The Undead. And his hellish child-Queen.

"They always come at night."

Had he spoken aloud? Taking a deep breath and a sip of water, he returned to his vigil at the window.

Perky sat right in the corner of the room, his back to the wall, watching the living-room door open slowly. Two shadows entered the room first, one large, one small.

The larger one was followed by Carl Smith. Dark, curly hair. Thick brow. Piggy eyes. Snub nose. Desperate Dan stubbled chin. Bull neck merging into a tight white singlet, like some latent-homosexual action hero. Impossibly tight jeans. Impossibly large trainers. He was followed by a tiny girl in a grey sweat suit. Hair pulled back in a Croydon facelift.. Huge hoop earrings. Jaw moving incessantly. Both figures had their arms folded.

Perky couldn't believe the girl. She looked more like eight than sixteen.

The two figures moved toward him slowly, their shadows engulfing and devouring him, silent save for the rumination of the girl.

"Congratulations," Perky heard himself say, rising to his feet equally slowly. "I hear you got married."

Neither Smith nor the girl answered but continued to creep forward.

"Congratulations again, Smithy. I hear you're a dad," continued Perky, trying to keep the knife in his belt, and the baseball bat behind his back. "Or you were a dad."

"I killed the baby," said the girl, little more than a baby herself.

Even as she said it, Perky realised that it was a diversionary tactic, and even as he realised, he knew that it had worked. His eyes flickered to the little girl, and Smith sprang forward.

Perky brought the bat forward and deflected Smith's blow. Smith's fist hit the wall behind him, and the attacker grunted in pain. Perky brought his right knee up swiftly and scored a direct hit. He couldn't believe his luck as Smith fell backward, squealing.

As Smith hit the floor, so Perky hit his head with the bat, hard. He felt the shock all the way up his arms. He struck again. And again.

The silly little girl tried to get between him and Smith, so he pushed her away, grinning as she fell over.

He returned to the task of hitting Smith's head as hard as he could over and over. Eventually, he was rewarded with a cracking sound. His elation grew as he watched the head disintegrate with each blow.

Finally, chest heaving, breath coming in great gasps, he leaned the sodden bat against the wall behind him and removed the knife from his belt. He knelt in front of Smith's remains.

A sound distracted him. What was it? Crying. A little child crying. He glanced at the girl. It was her. Sitting cross-legged and burbling "You killed him, you killed him," between sobs.

Perky became aware of the knife in his hand. The fact he was covered in a sticky liquid, black in the moonlight. He straightened up and blinked.

What had he done?

The little girl had tripled in age.

"You killed Sean," she sobbed.

STONES ARE BREATHING TONIGHT
Russell Hemmell

I met Ellen and Shaun in Canongate, in an Edinburgh devastated by the Iron Plague. When I first saw them, coming out of the South Grey's Close like ghouls from another age, I almost pulled the trigger. My hesitation saved us both—Ellen and me. She was on the point of shooting back.

Shaun laughed and walked in between us, extending his hand. "Peace and love, mate. It's not us you have to fear. Lower your gun. You too, Sis."

"I guess you're right," I conceded.

We shook hands, while Ellen acknowledged me with a nod.

I looked around, trying not to flinch at the view of the melted buildings among stumps of black stones half-eroded by inorganic decay and ignoring the stench coming from the ruins.

"Yes, here it's not any better," Shaun said with a smirk. "If you had expected the Old Town standing like it was in the old good days, you were having a fanciful dream."

Yes, and that was the awakening.

I sighed. It was going to be a long day.

*

Days were indeed unbearable long in the Scottish Summer –along with nights too short and troubled. I woke up

171

sweating, my hand ready on the gun near my pillow. The silvery titanium surface was cold between my fingers. And precious. Nothing else could be used any longer, for whatever artefact – civilian or military – because not just iron, as the moniker would have suggested, but most of the metals were vulnerable to the Iron Plague. Like humans or animals, and even some plants. A few creatures remained alive, sure, but that proved a mixed blessing, since they were rabid and famished. Damn dangerous for all the others. I considered myself no exception.

I gave a sidelong look at the two figures wrapped in blankets sleeping on the other side of the fire. After travelling alone for so long, I was glad to find survivors – healthy ones – even without actively searching for them, however many or few they could be. I had only tried to escape as far away as possible.

Images of doom that I had tried to push away without success crept back into my mind. We would have never forgotten that moment, 2325 days ago, when apocalypse came to us into the form of tiny stuff out of nowhere – nanoparticles of a technology turned badly wrong and, worse, alive on its own. The worst thing? Nobody knew the extent of that catastrophe, nor its scientific explanation. What remained was under the eyes of the ones who got away, looking like nightmares too persistent for sanity.

I went back to sleep. Nothing to gain by indulging in them.

*

"Raven? What the heck of a name is this?" Shaun said, while we were sharing a breakfast the morning after in one of Canongate's derelict houses.

"Mine, you *Shaun of the Dead*. Anything to say?"

He laughed and threw me a bottle. "Drink. Water in Edinburgh is not safe everywhere. This one is."

I grabbed it on the fly and drank. It had no taste, indication good enough there were no metal particles. I revelled in that simple pleasure, like a man lost in the desert sipping drops of oasis water he had searched for too long. Not a casual metaphor either.

"What have you found out about it?" Shaun said after a moment.

"The Plague, you mean?"

"Yes. You're from the South. You should have seen more of that in London than we had here."

"I guess so," I replied, trying hard to forget the accuracy of those details. "But we haven't discovered much either."

Ellen made a sign with her hands that Shaun translated for me.

"We?"

"Yes. The people I worked with. I am a biologist – or I should say, I was."

Shaun had not asked until that moment why somebody from a place several hundred miles away was strolling around in his city, when no form of transportation existed any longer. He asked no questions, and I had not explained. What for? Stories from the Plague were appallingly similar, and nobody had any tears left. Not even me. I couldn't cry any longer, apart from out of hunger pangs.

"Has it happened in the same way?"

"I wouldn't know. I wasn't here." I said. "But from what I could see, pretty much."

"Which metals are affected the most?"

"As far as I know, all metals except the platinum

group and titanium – don't ask me why. Some of them more than others, of course. Only old stones and wood remain unmelted, even though structures made up with high concentration of the most vulnerable minerals in their bricks have collapsed too. This explains the ruins here, and the fact they are not uniform."

Shaun nodded, looking around. "What about contagion?"

"That depends on the minerals of the water people drank. They might be lucky or not. In London, we weren't." I thought again at the delay we had discovered that and how long it took us to find a remedy. Looking at the statistics too long. Half of the population was infected by then, and the images of the sick created a new category of clinical horror. Ebola was a mild cold in comparison, even though it bore some resemblance in terms of symptoms.

"After a while it didn't make any difference."

"No. Not for us. And not for any other living beings on planet Earth."

Iron. Iron is the key of the problem, I mused in silence. There are four stable isotopes in iron. It has taken an awful lot of time before realising only one of them, the rarest of all, was somehow more resistant to the degenerative particles. Having known it in advance, maybe some preventive measures could have been taken, infrastructures maintained, lives saved... "Plants – many plants adapted to survive without, or used the more resistant isotope: we didn't know until the end, and now I wonder..." I said, cutting short a long line of reasoning.

"About what?"

"If this was a punishment for what we have done to this planet. The hubris of the Ancient Greeks, you know, that attracts nemesis. If plants have started to recover, maybe one day the whole planet will. Except us, the real virus, eliminated forever for the better good."

"Whatever you say, mate. Personally, I don't know anything about your Greeks, past or present." Shaun shrugged. "But if I were you, I wouldn't be overly concerned about any future day."

"Why?"

"We might not live to see one. Come on, let's go exploring Meadows."

"Have you not given up the search for survivors?" I already knew the answer.

"No. This is how we found you, wasn't it?"

We suited up and walked toward a gaping hole that once was a prime residential area of the city, something I could still remember from my high school travel days. I braced for the cringing sight I knew awaited me there.

I was not deluded.

*

As if Meadows had not been enough, a couple of weeks later I was in for a treat: the core of the Old Town, the Castle itself.

"Clear," Shaun said, his wooden torch casting a cone of light into the half-collapsed corridor. Flames and shadows made the old castle frightening even to my jaded eyes.

We had waited a few days preparing as much as we could for the exploration of the dungeons and the rest of the subterraneans. It was the last thing we had left to do before moving out of the city and going to the countryside. It was not accidental. I dreaded what we would find, and yet I decided to accompany them, fighting my resistance.

While we were sure nobody and nothing could possibly live in what remained of the upper floors, the basement and below were most likely standing, even if in a badly damaged fashion. If there's anything still alive in Edinburgh, it is here it's going to be. And it won't be pretty. I repeated the words to myself, trying to keep my head cold and my senses sharp.

Ellen moved forward, silent and attentive.

"Careful," I said to her. "We don't know what awaits us there."

"Sis can't hear you, Raven," Shaun reminded me gently.

I kept forgetting Ellen could only read my lips. She showed nothing of the typical hesitation of disabled people when put into unfamiliar environments. I guess because in that hell she was more at ease than us.

"Don't worry for her." He smiled with pride. "What she can't hear, she can smell."

And it was true. A few metres later, she gestured for us to stop and got onto her knees, examining the lurid path, mired with rain filtered from the upper levels and debris. Then she turned, looking at her brother and signing.

"Stones were breathing here," he said.

"What?" I wasn't sure I'd understood him.

"This place was inhabited. Ellen detects an animal presence," he said. "But she can't tell if there's anything still around, dead or alive. The stench is strong but not unbearable."

"There might be something alive. Maybe even humans."

"Or what they have turned into," Shaun said.

"You don't believe they've become zombies, do you?" That was one of the rumours, at the beginning.

And for a simple reason. It would have actually been reassuring, considering that a few governments did have a zombie contingency plan, as fanciful as that sounded.

He shook his head. "No such luck. Sick and demented, yes. Nowhere less dangerous, maybe more."

"Certainly more. Before London went still, there were a few massacres." I looked around, trying to guess what was lurking beyond the entrance of the vaulted chambers of the dungeons.

Ellen stopped, extending her arm to keep us from proceeding. She signalled something to Shaun and leapt alone inside the chamber.

"What is she doing?" I wasn't happy she'd disappeared.

"She has sensed something."

"One more reason to join her."

"No. If there's anybody there, it's in the obscurity. She can perceive it quicker than we can hear it, let alone react. Trust her, mate." He stared into my eyes. "Without Ellen, I wouldn't be alive."

I waited, impatiently, for something to happen, amazed by Shaun's attitude. My fingers kept fidgeting nervously on the stock of my gun.

The wait wasn't long. After ten minutes or so, her slim silhouette emerged out of the dark pool in front of us. I searched for her expression in the shadow, or to understand what she was communicating to her brother, but I relaxed.

"What did she say?"

"That whatever was breathing here before has already left. Not long since. Everything on the ground is dead. Only animals, for what she could see."

This sounded as a good moment for us to leave as well. There was nothing to be gained by hanging around a graveyard, regardless of its historical merit.

"Do you know the most terrifying thing about having hordes of sick people chasing us?"

Shaun asked the question, pensive.

"I am sure you're going to tell me." I knew he couldn't help himself.

"That there's no one else normal," he said. "What if there's simply nobody else in this city or on the whole goddamn planet who hasn't been infected?"

That was a thought I was not ready to entertain. "Let's go," I said, turning on my heels.

"Wait. I still want to explore," Shaun said. "I'll see you at the World's End, mate."

"You mean the place, right?"

"Where else?" Shaun snickered. "For the rest, the world ended long ago."

I walked out of the dungeons, creeping up from the half-collapsed stairs and helping my ascent with ropes. There was an uncomfortable feeling of failure niggling inside me. Somehow, I was sure the twins were feeling the same way.

We can't admit it, even with ourselves, but we hoped for those marauders. We were alert and ready for battle. Yes, even willing. Nothing is worse than being alone, not even death. But alone we are. We have explored the whole Midlothian County, and haven't been able to find a single, breathing creature. The truth? There's nobody else here.

*

The world did end long ago, Shaun was right. Or at least the Scottish portion of the world. We had the confirmation a few days after the Castle's episode, on a sunny afternoon when Ellen came to search for us.

"There's a trail," Shaun interpreted for me.

"Which kind of trail?"

"She's not sure. But there were traces of something alive, and they lead to a place outside the city."

Ellen led us across Leith Walk to what, before the Plague, used to be one of Edinburgh's seaside suburbs. And it was there that, just a dozen metres away from the shore, we had an amazing view. The sand was littered with corpses – animals of all forms, species and dimensions. There were hundreds of thousands of them, covering the beach past where our stare could follow, and probably further. It looked to me as if, in a sort of hivemind instinct, they had tried to escape en masse from the ravaging disease to a safer place and had been stopped by the sea. Some of them were bloated with water. An evident sign they all died in the attempt of swimming.

Shaun and I did not say a word. Ellen knelt on the ground and cried.

*

That same night, when we were sitting outside looking at the sky – a pastime we seemed unable to get rid of, Iron Plague or not, Shaun caught me following Ellen with my regard.

"What are you waiting for, Raven?"

"Excuse me?"

"That day in the dungeons... I have seen you."

"So?"

"You were worried, mate," he continued. "You fancy her."

"Correct."

"Bummer! And I thought you had a crush on me." Shaun laughed.

"I could, if I had not met her."

"Well, sincere condolences. Ellen was not dating anybody even before the Plague, when she had quite a choice." He smiled. "I guess the shortage of breathing preys has not changed a thing for her."

I was not surprised. I shrugged.

"But she likes you, I feel it. I know my sister," he continued with a smile. "You should ask her out. She can't talk, but she would make herself understood nonetheless."

I nodded slowly. "I will."

*

But I didn't. Not that day, not any time after. I preferred living side by side to the woman I loved, adoring her in silence rather than risking her refusal or, worse, being sent away. That was something I could not bear. I could not live alone any longer.

We kept doing what we did since had met, searching for survivors, of whatever kind. Not trying to find not a solution –there was probably none – for a cause that had lost any relevance to us. What we wanted was just a reason to remain alive.

Days became weeks and then months.

We travelled looking at our stars, in a sky often clouded.

*

"Do you need assistance, Fidra? Have you fed the dogs?"

"No, Raven. Ellen will help me."

After one year or so of roaming a desolate, silent Scotland, we eventually found a place in which stones were still breathing – the remote island of Fidra in the East Lothian, where a derelict church was preserved almost intact. A young girl with two dogs lived there. She couldn't have been older than seven. God only knows how she had survived or arrived at that place. She didn't remember a great deal, apart from her parents taking her to that place and then dying of the same disease that claimed the rest of the world.

She is with us now. She has no memory of her name either, so we called her Fidra, out of the place we found her. She's especially attached to Ellen, and the two are inseparable. But we all love her, and not only because she's adorable and the only other survivor we have found so far. She has given us hope.

Now we know the Iron Plague is not the end.

Maybe it was in Scotland, in Europe, in the advanced world. But not for the entire Earth. Somewhere on this planet, people like us with strange genetic disorders that metabolise iron in their blood in a different way, are still alive. And if they are, they will be living with nature. Not in metal structures but in wood huts and underground caves. It is from them that civilisation will be built again, one more in harmony with life.

Us? After our long tour across Scotland, we returned to Edinburgh, settling in this Canongate melted and stinking, but where millenary dark stones stand stubborn. I guess history made them resilient in the first place and keeps them alive. And they're going to live on, longer than us. But we offer our contribution: we make them breathing.

*

It's only 4:45 am, but at this latitude dawn is already breaking.

I look around at our room made of plastic and synthetic scraps. We sleep on a pallet of straws and rags. Sometimes there's only enough for Fidra to eat while we rely on berries and weird looking but edible sprouts.

Later in the morning we will go fishing into a loch. Ellen thinks life is returning in the countryside. She has seen flies near the water, and possibly there's something brewing there. We are all excited at that perspective.

I take Shaun's hand while he's still asleep, and I put it on my breast. He squeezes it a little, and without waking up he starts making love to me. I have no illusion he feels real attraction, but, as he said once, only Ellen has not been affected by the lack of available mates. To me, it makes no difference. It's an animal instinct that needs to be satisfied, a species that has to survive and if thanks to our lust we can generate one precious life for a depopulated land, that's something good for everybody.

I allow him to pleasure me and I close my eyes. This day's going to be as long as the others, but it's a promising one.

WINTER OF DISCONTENT
Stephanie Ellis

"Call it Youth Opportunities," said Terry. "You've got the youth and I see the opportunity."

"Where?" asked Gary, eying the abandoned factory grounds sceptically.

"Here, this little beaut is about to become a gold mine, courtesy of our Scouse brothers."

Again Terry looked blankly at the depressing scene. He had absolutely no idea what his uncle was on about.

"But you were closed down, Health 'n Safety," said Gary, looking at the factory that had once churned out bits of plastic whose purpose he had never known even when his uncle had given him a Saturday job there.

"Yeah, well, this time all we're doin' is a bit of storage. And our customers 'aint exactly picky about their surroundings." Terry thrust a copy of *The Daily Mirror* into Gary's hands. Gary had avoided the papers; with their incessant pictures of uncollected piles of rubbish and marching strikers they had made pretty depressing reading. He could see nothing in the current headline that could possibly be the reason for his uncle's good mood.

"There," said Terry, jabbing a picture with his stubby finger.

Gary looked again. Under a headline of '*Unable to Rest in Peace*', the picture showed row after row of coffins, like a girl on a Saturday night, the occupants were all dressed up with nowhere to go. And that wasn't the end of it. As Liverpool's gravediggers continued their strike, the city's morgues had reached capacity; here, the dead that had not yet reached the undertaker, had merely an anonymous black body bag to cover their indignity and were being piled up in a manner guaranteed to cause distress to the families left behind – if they knew.

"So…" said Gary.

"I've got a warehouse the council can use. Far enough away from prying eyes, reasonable rates. We can make a killing," said Terry, rubbing his hands together in greedy expectation.

A poor choice of words, thought Gary, looking at his uncle and the pictures of the unburied dead with equal amounts of distaste.

"Right," said Terry, "time to get to work. I think Warehouse Three would provide the best accommodation for our guests."

He unlocked the gate and Gary drove his uncle's old Cortina through. The car's suspension groaned slightly as Terry clambered into the passenger seat and allowed his nephew to bump and jolt him over the rutted tracks that wove their way between the disused factory and its sentinel warehouses until finally they arrived at Number Three.

The storage barn sat squat, grey and isolated at the far side of the industrial site. A chain-link fence swayed miserably behind it.

"Better fix that before anyone comes sniffing around," said Terry jerking his head in its direction.

Gary nodded; already certain it would be only one of God knows how many jobs his uncle was sure to pile on his shoulders. And they hadn't even discussed money yet. He looked at the warehouse, its two dark little windows piggy eyes on either side of a firmly closed mouth.

"Come on then, lad," said Terry. "Time to open shop."

It took the two of them to drag the big delivery doors to the old loading bay apart. Like a child at the dentist keeping its teeth firmly clamped together, the warehouse resisted their efforts for some time. But eventually, although still creaking in protest, it yielded, and the two men were able to enter the building.

Gary hopefully flipped up the light switches and was pleasantly surprised when the fluorescent strips crackled into life.

"Got our Derek to hook us up to the grid," said Terry, smirking.

Another shortcut, thought Gary, wondering how long it would take the Electricity Board to track down this drain on the nation's already overstretched resources. Better bring in some candles, just in case.

Then he tried the air-conditioning unit. It remained silent.

"Don't worry," said Terry. "If they're not in coffins, they're in special heat-sealed bags. You won't smell a thing. And it's pretty cold anyway…"

So candles, sleeping bag, thermals… and a bit of booze, just to take the edge off things.

"Right then, to work," said Terry, gesturing to the two forklifts sitting quietly in the corner of the warehouse.

For the next couple of hours, both men worked hard, moving out all the remaining debris from the racks and dumping it unceremoniously inside the disused factory. Old pallets, shreds of cardboard, mouldy rat poison, all was swept up or lifted down and hidden from view. Occasionally the lights flickered, and Gary thought they were going to give out but thankfully they remained on and they were able to get the job completed. He paused before he pulled the doors to again, the lights were off and the sight of that gaping darkness unsettled him in a way he had never felt before. He shrugged off his sense of foreboding and padlocked the doors, which now swung easily together.

"Ready to go then, Tel?" asked Morrison the following day. The councillor gazed round the warehouse with a look of relief. Basic but clean, remote and secure, the answer to all his problems. "And your capacity? You're sure you can cope?"

"We can take a thousand if we have to," said Terry.

"I hope it won't come to that," said Morrison. "This dispute can't go on much longer."

Terry shot his nephew a quick smile. Friends in the union had told them in no uncertain terms they would hold out as long as they had to – the public could always dig their own graves. But everybody knew that was unlikely to happen, people were invariably squeamish around death.

"I'll be sending the deliveries at night," said Morrison. "Don't want to spook anyone."

You don't want headlines either, thought Gary.

"And you've got security?"

"Put my own nephew on the job," said Terry as Gary stepped forward.

"Not quite how a young man would want to spend the night," said Morrison, giving Gary a sympathetic look.

"Oh, our Gary's a tough lad. Not easily scared, handy when he has to be," said Terry.

With the inspection over, Terry and Gary remained to take receipt of their first delivery. They sat in the small

186

office Terry had kitted out with an oil-heater, old black-and-white TV, and a pile of dubious magazines. Behind them the warehouse waited.

The rumble of an engine alerted them to the approach of their new customers. Terry handed Gary the driver's manifest.

"There you are, lad. They're all tagged, bagged and ready to go."

Gary hoisted the first bodies somewhat unceremoniously onto the forklift, his distaste evident as he drove past his uncle and into the far recesses of the store. But he performed the task efficiently, he did after all need the money, and soon the empty bays had been filled with the black-shrouded corpses. When the final one had been shelved securely, Terry signed the delivery form and watched the lorry driver disappear out of the gates.

"That's it for tonight," said Terry. "Remember, you only need to take a quick look around the premises once in a while. Can't for the life of me imagine anyone getting up to no good around here but you never know, we might get a sneaky reporter trying for a story."

Gary watched his uncle drive off and then locked the site's gates against whoever had the misfortune to be out that night. The man would be back in the morning to relieve his nephew for a few hours but until then, it was just Gary and the dead.

He switched on his torch, swinging it round in an arc, its beam capturing the sparkle of a frost that already lay heavily on the ground; above him, the night sky had taken on the tell-tale sludgy peach tint of clouds carrying a new delivery of snow. Gary only gave the other buildings a cursory glance. Their distorted shapes and silent abandonment made him feel uneasy. Even his company of the dead was preferable to his current position. Gary sped up and walked swiftly back to Warehouse Three. Its windows watched his approach and the door was already open to welcome him back. He could've sworn he'd shut it. As he stepped through, he pulled it firmly behind him, heard the latch fall into place.

His hand reached for the light switch but something stayed him; it wouldn't do to attract the attention of anyone living just over from the estate. They might query a warehouse's lights being on in the middle of the night, call the police. But would it matter if they did? He wasn't doing anything illegal after all. His uncle though had been more than clear about avoiding unwanted visitors. So Gary walked between the endless bays with only the small beam of his torch to light the way, past the empty shelves towards the occupants sleeping soundly in their endless night.

As he walked amongst them he heard an occasional scratching and rustling, caught slight movements from the corner of his eye but when he swung his torch round to investigate, there was nothing. Rats, he thought grimly. He'd get his uncle to buy some more poison tomorrow. Wouldn't do to return the corpses with nibbled toes. The image it conjured up made him giggle, the giggle became a laugh and soon he was convulsed in a tidal wave of merriment as he made his way back to the office. He discarded his gloves and overcoat and settled himself in the slightly tatty armchair, enjoying the warmth of the oil-heater and allowing himself, at last, a small scotch. The chair reclined slightly under his weight, and that with the heat and the alcohol, soon sent him into a deep sleep. His chest rose easily, his heart beat steadily even as the skitterings and scratchings grew in volume in the unit behind him. The heater continued to generate a comfortable warmth, even as the temperature plunged amongst the bays of dead who shifted complainingly beneath this fresh assault on their dignity. They only hushed when a voice whispered its lullaby to them in the darkness. Then, like Gary, they too slept.

The blare of a horn woke Gary from his sleep. A dim light made its way through the frost-crusted window. The oil-heater had gone out and his bones were stiff and aching from the cold. He had only just got to his feet when the door swung open and Terry appeared in front of him.

"'Ere you go, lad," he said. "Hot coffee and a bacon sarnie."

Gary banged his hands together to try and get the circulation going but it took some time before he could bend his fingers enough to take hold of the proffered cup, let alone eat the roll. Eventually though he could feel life return and once Terry had got the heater working again, he began to feel a bit more human.

"Shouldn't let that go out, lad," said Terry, indicating the heater. "Don't want you ending up as stiff as that lot in there. I'll bring round some more oil later, perhaps a few extra blankets. Now, anything to report?"

Gary shook his head.

"Well I'll just take a quick look out back and then you can go home. Get yourself a hot bath or something. You don't look that good."

Gary watched his uncle disappear into the recesses, tried to stamp out the numbness that was still clinging stubbornly to his body, refusing to let go its grip.

His uncle reappeared in the office, a slightly puzzled look on his face. He rooted around the paperwork on the desk.

"What you lookin' for?" asked Gary.

"Yesterday's delivery note."

"Why?"

"I don't know. Might be my eyes playing tricks on me in my old age but it's just that, just that there seem to be more bodies in there than I thought."

"More?"

"Yeah."

The two men went into the back of the warehouse, both counted the number of corpses on the shelves, both came to the same number. The same as the number on the delivery note. But Terry had been right. There definitely seemed to be more bodies on the shelves, more body bags anyway.

"Count again," said Terry.

They recounted and again came up with the same number. Terry rubbed his eyes. "Must be a trick of the light," he said eventually. "Come on, let's lock this place up and get out of here for a bit. I've got Ron to bring his dogs down. They'll look after things for us."

As he sat in his uncle's car, Gary finally felt the numbness inside seep away. He really would have to make sure he kept warmer the next night.

"How many this time?" Terry asked the driver.

"Another fifty. That brings you up to one hundred and fifty now." The driver looked at the doors which led into the darkness. "Rather you than me, mate," he said to Gary. "Would creep me out, place like this."

Terry and Gary made quick work of loading up the bays. The cold was already creeping back in and the driver wanted to get away as quickly as possible.

"Right then, lad," said Terry. "Got everything you want? I've put a couple of oil canisters round the back in case you need more for the heater – don't want to break any Health and Safety regulations by having them inside.

Your aunt gave me a few more blankets for you, oh and she's done a bit of baking as well. Anything else?"

"What about the dogs?"

"Oh, Ron said he'd collect them in an hour or two. It's a bit late but he's got a delivery of his own to make. Said he'd pick them up on his way back."

"What if I have to go out there in the meantime?"

"Oh, they're pussycats really. You'll be fine. Here."

Terry gave Gary a box of *Goodboy Choc Drops*. "He says they're partial to these."

Gary did not feel reassured.

"Tell you what," said Terry. "I'll lock up the main gate when I go, save you having to come out. Then you don't need to do a patrol until Ron comes."

Before he could even ask how he was supposed to let the man in with the dogs on the loose, Terry had made a dash for the door. The sound of dogs barking accompanied the rumble of Terry's car as he headed towards the exit.

Gary decided not to think about it. Let his uncle get out of that one. He wasn't the one who was going to be stuck here all night. He rubbed his fist against the window, smearing open a peephole that lasted only long enough to show the first flakes of snow drifting down. He picked up his trusty torch and went back into the warehouse, its spotlight picking out the newly filled bays alongside those from the day before. He shook his head slightly at the sight. What he saw and what he counted still didn't add up. Despite his reluctance, he decided to do several laps of the warehouse in an effort to keep his muscles warm. As he walked, his steps evened out into a regular march.

"Left, right, left, right," he intoned as he drilled himself along the aisles. "About turn, hup two, three, four, hup, two, three, four."

He'd only lasted a couple of months in the cadets and here he was three years later, stomping around the warehouse like a professional soldier. His cadet leader would be so proud if he could see him now. See him now. Gary stopped. Took in his surroundings. Started to laugh. The old bugger had been right, had said he'd never amount to much. A rustling sound caught his attention, drew him to the back of the warehouse. Shadows shifted behind him. He walked on. There was a scratching now, like nails on metal, a low growling. It was coming from outside. He swung his beam along the back wall. Noticed an old fire escape. He'd completely forgotten about that. He tucked the torch under his arm and slowly pressed the bars of the door down. Gary peered through the crack and saw two pairs of orange eyes turn towards him. The dogs. They started to growl. Then suddenly the door whipped itself out of his hands, opened wide to make him the perfect target for the canine monsters but instead of coming for him, they backed away. Their bodies shrunk to the ground, the hair on their backs on end, pathetic whimpers escaping their retreating forms. Gary stepped forward but the dogs backed away even more.

"Pussycats," he laughed. "Terry's right about that."

He caught sight of the canisters next to the door. The extra fuel his uncle had brought. Wouldn't harm to take one in now. He had to put his torch in his pocket to drag it into the warehouse. It meant he didn't notice how much the dark had grown beyond anything he, or any other man had ever seen. He closed the fire exit doors and continued to drag the drum back towards his office. He left it at the end of the nearest bay. He wasn't so stupid that he'd store it near the heater in his room. Again he settled himself down, thoroughly cocooned this time by all the extra blankets and with the heater set at full blast. He allowed himself a small whisky – it was becoming a ritual – and found an old film to watch on the telly. He was soon fast asleep.

In the warehouse, the temperature dropped even lower than it had the previous night. Complaints were heard as bodies turned uncomfortably in their sleep until they were hushed again by that strange lullaby. The softly sung words made their way to the edge of Gary's subconscious and his mind strained to listen so that his dreams filled themselves with bizarre images of frozen wastes and dead men walking, dogs howling as fire consumed them, but it did not wake him.

This time it wasn't the blare of a horn that woke him but a firm hand shaking him awake.

"Gary, Gary, come on now lad, up and at 'em."

Terry stood above him, his smile holding a slight look of concern. "Fire's gone out again," he said, indicating the heater. "You're beginning to look like our customers in there."

Gary groaned and forced his body round into a more upright position. His limbs felt heavy and wooden. They rebelled against the instructions his brain was currently sending to them, fought against his desire to get up and moving. They just wanted to lie there, to rest in peace.

"Drink this," said Terry. He poured out a cup of coffee from the Thermos and added a dash of scotch to it. "That'll get your circulation going."

While Gary forced himself into some sort of life, Terry went into the warehouse, checked the occupants as before.

"Certainly cold back there," he said cheerfully. "That'll definitely keep any smell down. Think we could do with another tally on the numbers though."

Gary followed Terry into the back of the warehouse, noticing how Terry had opened the doors as wide as possible.

"Delivery'll be coming soon," he said by way of explan-ation. "And it'll give us more light."

"What happened to deliveries only at night?" Gary asked.

Terry shrugged but Gary knew his uncle didn't like examining dead bodies in the dark, that such things made him nervous, or perhaps he just didn't like the cold. On all scores, Gary was in whole-hearted agreement with him.

They both counted up individually and compared results, still one hundred and fifty but Gary could've sworn there were more on the shelves.

"Blame the cold, and the whisky," he laughed. Terry nodded but still looked doubtful.

"Ron bringing his dogs back?" asked Gary as they made their way to the car.

Before Terry could answer, the phone rang in the office.

"That was Ron," he said. "Apologised for not picking the dogs up last night, said he'll come by in a bit and collect them."

They looked at each other.

"I didn't see the dogs when I came in," said Terry. "I assumed he'd taken them. When did you last see them?"

"Last night," said Gary, explaining about their attempts to get into the warehouse and subsequent retreat.

"Odd," mused Terry. "Let's take a look."

Gary led him around the back of the warehouse, both men keeping a wary eye open just in case the mutts should reappear, even as they both felt deep down that the dogs were nowhere around.

"Here," said Gary, pointing to the faint traces the dogs had left in the snow. Shallow grooves showed where their bellies had dragged along the ground, where their nails had scrabbled on the cold surface. Another deeper groove outlined the path Gary had taken with the oil drum back into the warehouse.

"What's this?" asked Terry, pointing to some strange marks made roughly behind where Gary had been standing. Slivers of snow had been channelled out of the ground, as if someone had scraped their nails over its pristine surface.

Gary shrugged his shoulders, could not remember anything apart from dragging the canister inside. That was all it could've been.

"Come on," said Terry. "Let's follow these and see if we can find those damned animals."

"And if we do?"

"I've got the choc drops," laughed Terry, but there was no humour in his eyes.

They followed the dogs' trail. It led them from the warehouse towards the old factory. The markings had changed shape by this time, the animals no longer slinking along but running, hasty paw prints churning up the snow in mini flurries. Gary could see it all now, how they had run, how they had howled, bolted into the factory whose doors had swung open ready to receive them, watched as they scrabbled to the top of the debris dumped there earlier by his uncle and himself, yelped and roared with pain as the fire was lit beneath them.

"Gary, Gary, you alright, lad?"

His uncle was stood at his shoulder, watching him with a puzzled expression.

"Yeah, I'm ok," he said and held his breath as Terry opened the factory doors. The rubbish tip was still there,

there was no fire or the smell of one and there were no dogs. He felt almost relieved.

"Nothing," said Terry after they'd poked around for a good hour. "Strange."

They returned outside, closed the factory once more.

"Terry Jefferson, you bastard." The roar echoed around the site.

"Ron? What the…?"

Gary and Terry hurried back to the warehouse. Its doors were ajar, and Ron Goodman stood glowering at the entrance. "I lent you my dogs in good faith and you… you…"

"I don't understand," said Terry.

"What don't you understand?" said Ron, grabbing hold of Terry and pulling him into the darkness of the warehouse. "What don't you understand about that?"

All three men were now at the entrance to the aisle containing the previous night's deliveries. Black shapes cloaked the shelves and lying amongst them were the bodies of the two dogs.

"Come on now, Ron," said Terry. "What'd you take me for? Couldn't get near those monsters of yours, nor could our Gary. They'd've bit our arm off first. And look, there's not a scratch on them."

The men moved closer, noticed the absence of any wounds, the stiffness of the bodies from cold, the strange light in their eyes.

"Gary saw them last night outside when he was getting the oil drum in, perhaps they got in then," offered Terry. "Looks like they froze to death."

It was the only logical explanation although Gary was convinced they had not slipped past him. But considering the look on Ron's face he wasn't going to argue the toss. The big man looked close to tears.

"These were good dogs," he said. "If I thought for one minute..."

"No, no," said Terry. "Unfortunate accident, that's all it could've been, eh Gary?"

"Yeah," said Gary. "Unfortunate accident."

Ron still looked doubtful but appeared to accept their explanation. "I'll have to leave them here for the moment, you do realise that don't you?"

"Eh?" said Terry.

"I want to give them a decent burial but the ground's too hard. If I leave them here they'll be alright, won't decompose none either."

"I'm not sure," said Terry.

"We could cover them with a tarp. No one'd notice and who'd complain? This lot? You owe me that at least, after all, I was doing you a favour."

Terry nodded. "Yeah, you're right, the least we could do. And what's two more amongst this lot anyway?"

They locked up the warehouse behind them and headed home for the day. They had decided to risk leaving the place unguarded, just this once. Give it a day or two before they asked Ron if they could borrow a couple more of his dogs.

Gary spent most of the day dozing in front of the fire. Songs from the radio intermittently filtered through to his dreams but mostly he was listening to the lullaby from the previous night. He was beginning to find it soothing, familiar. It helped him sleep.

"Don't know what's got into you," said Terry, as he shook his nephew awake yet again. "Sleep all night and now all day. So much for the energy of youth."

Gary tried to smile but found his mouth wouldn't stretch in the right direction. In fact, nothing much seemed to want to move the way it was supposed to.

His uncle practically had to support him all the way to the car, ignoring Gary's mother's worried look. "Just for another night, Lizzie," Terry promised. "Then I'll do a stint."

That seemed to satisfy her but when Gary turned to wave at her from the window, he could see the anxiety etched deep on her face. He pulled the passenger visor down and examined his own features in the mirror. His skin was deathly white and his lips carried a bluish tinge. The cold was getting to him more than he thought. But Terry had promised him a night off tomorrow. The song playing on the radio seemed to echo his thoughts, *Just One More Night...*

The delivery that day was for thirty. Now they were home to one hundred and eighty dead souls and two dead dogs. Terry left Gary with a full bottle of scotch that night. Told him not to worry about going outside. To stay inside and keep as warm as possible. Only if he heard something really strange was he to investigate.

Gary nodded obediently. Despite his uncle's tendency to go for the fast money, he cared about his nephew and Gary knew that his mother's expression had tugged at his conscience.

"Besides," said Terry. "It's not as though they haven't got a couple of guard dogs in there now."

They had both laughed uncomfortably at that. Then Terry had gone, and Gary was once more on his own. He wrapped himself up and picked up his torch, determined to do at least one inspection before retiring to the office, regardless of what his uncle had said.

He stepped into the warehouse and walked down the first bay. Its entire length was now full but there were still several other bays to hold any future deliveries. The sheer volume of what you could only call death made the atmosphere feel heavy, oppressive. Gary tried to shake it off and stepped up his pace. It brought him to where the two dogs were... or had been. They were no longer there. And at the far end of the aisle he now saw four glowing eyes. They'd made a mistake. They couldn't be dead. Slowly he started to back up, retrace his route to the office. The soft padding of the animals' feet followed him. He tried to run but his cumbersome outerwear tripped him up and he fell over. The dogs were nearer now, the safety of the office further away. In desperation he looked at the shelving behind him. The bodies lay silently, unaware of the commotion going on around them. He clambered up, apologising as he did so for stepping on frozen arms and legs, wincing as he heard the occasional snap of a bone breaking beneath his weight. He didn't know how he managed it but soon he was on the third shelf up, a long way from the ground, and thankfully the dogs, who now leapt and growled at its base, their eyes glowing red in the pitch.

In despair, he realised he was trapped, at least until his uncle came back in the morning. And it was so cold. It surely hadn't been that cold on the previous nights? And he needed to keep warm. He took his torch out and swung it along his perch, noted the rising and falling of the wave of black stored on the shelf. At least they seemed warm and cosy. Then he looked to his left. An empty body bag lay there. Why? Probably just a spare when they unloaded, tossed up and forgotten about. Perhaps there were more empties, perhaps they were responsible for the discrepancies in the numbers.

His finger ran idly along the zip, felt the metal teeth part easily beneath his touch. Inside was a cocoon of darkness, inviting. Without thinking, he slipped inside, pulled the zip up to his chin, his nose, stopping at his eyes. He didn't want to be completely wrapped in black, although considering his surroundings it wouldn't make much difference either way. He turned his torch off. The dogs stopped growling. Everything went quiet for a while.

Gary must've dozed off. It couldn't have been long for as far as he could see it was still night-time. He heard, no, sensed, movement. All around him there was a general stirring, a muttering.

Someone was walking between the aisles, not the dogs, not his uncle, not... he peered over the edge... anything he could name. The shadow was dragging something behind him. It looked just like the body bags that Gary now lay amongst except that this one moved, and it not only moved but writhed, hissing like a snake. The shape stopped opposite Gary and tossed the squirming bag onto the bay. It lay still for a moment and then started to spread, merging itself into its companions, spreading the darkness, adding the extra weight that Gary and his uncle had noticed when they had tried to count the number of the dead that occupied the shelves.

The hissing had stopped, replaced by something that seemed to suck and pull, tear and bite – the sounds of someone, something feeding. The cold Gary had kept at bay for so long, seeped back in; even the bag seemed to offer no protection this time. He tried to suppress his shivering, pulled himself deeper inside his shroud without attracting the attention of the shape that had now moved on to the next bay, dragging another black-cased serpent with it. Again it was tossed up amongst the occupants. Then it started to walk back down Gary's side. It stopped. And laughed.

"Now is the winter of our discontent," it roared in a mocking parody of Shakespeare's infamous play. "But man's winter is my summer and has given me a ripe harvest. So much bounty for my armies to feed on, so many sins to be eaten and nurtured, tithes that must be paid."

Gary could see eyes glowing red in the depths of the shadow, fought to tell himself that the cold was playing tricks on his mind, that he would wake up soon and all would be normal once more. He closed his eyes and opened them again, found nothing had changed. He wasn't dreaming and those burning eyes were now looking at him.

"Ah, my young caretaker. What a pleasant surprise." The voice was strangely gentle, soothing. "I do so like to meet those who work for me, in the flesh, so to speak."

Gary just stared. He had the feeling he'd met this man, this creature before. He forced himself to focus but the image in front of him kept blurring. He saw Morrison, his uncle, Ron, the massed crowd of the GMWU on the streets, even himself. Their eyes, their faces, they were all there merging with his own projected features into a collage he couldn't make sense of.

"You see, don't you?" it whispered. "Yourself, the world, all that greed, hate, envy, it all writes itself on me and I eat it up, gobble it up like those prized turkeys you stuffed yourself with not so long ago at Christmas. And I have dined well this winter on the fury of the little man, on his spite and ingratitude, on all those ugly emotions borne of misplaced pride, recruited so many wavering souls and this is where I take delivery." A claw-like hand gestured to the aisles around them. "But you need your sleep boy and I still have much work to do. We will continue our chat another time… perhaps."

Gary felt waves of tiredness roll over him, melting away the fear that had kept him frozen awake. Strong hands tucked him tighter into his cocoon, pulled the zip up further, over his chin, his nose, his eyes.

"Hush," crooned the shadow from the darkness. "Hush oh hush, your monster calls. Hush, oh hush, the dark must fall."

Another writhing bag was tossed up on the shelf, this time next to Gary. He did not feel its weight, did not appreciate the extra warmth as it coiled itself around him.

"Dead to the world," laughed the shadow as he left the boy behind him, stepping out into the ice-hearted landscape to continue his night's work.

The warehouse stilled, settled into silence once more. A paramedic on a motorway zipped up a drunk driver, a mortician shrouded a fallen priest, a vagrant pulled a blanket over the face of his companion and walked away, leaving him to sleep alone on the streets.

A full truck pulled up outside Warehouse Three the next day. It stood silent, waiting.

"That no-good nephew of yours done a bunk?" laughed the driver.

"Looks like it," growled Terry.

He'd track him down soon enough, of that he was sure and then he'd give him hell to pay. In the meantime, it looked as though he would be on duty here. He shelved the new arrivals, signed the manifest and settled himself down with the scotch Gary had left behind. Slowly the temperature began to drop and the darkness within the warehouse grew.

THE ADELPHI
Alyson Faye

It's not easy being the youngest. Becca was always being left out or left behind. It wasn't fair.

She so wanted to be in. Especially with them. So when Jake and Joss had laughingly challenged everyone to the "hugest dare ever," Becca had been the first in the gang to leap up and accept. Now she was sorry. Sorry seven times over. Joss had nearly choked with amusement on her chewing gum, while Jake had smirked behind his usual fag.

"OK Titch," he'd said, shrugging. "You're on."

Then he had bent down and whispered into Becca's ear. Her bones had melted and she'd had to hold onto her bladder.

Bastards! she thought, *you 100 percent bastards!*

Two nights later Becca sneaked out of her family's tiny, terraced house, with its clutchy, grimy curtains, and began hiking out of town along the main road towards the destination of the 'dare'.

"We'll know if you bottle it, Titch," Jake had warned her, waving his lighted ciggy close to her face and smirking when she'd backed away.

She'd spotted him spying on her from his bedroom window when she'd strolled past his foster parent's house. Keeping his beady on her. So, to show him she'd waved. He'd laughed and given her the finger. She hadn't dared to do the same.

Ten minutes of walking onto the outskirts of the town, Becca faced the crumbling Adelphi; a once regal hotel, now derelict. Its state of decay didn't deter the local kids, druggies and the homeless from creeping inside its rotten shell. Looking up at its façade Becca felt dwarfed. It had been such a grand old behemoth. She noticed the pair of stone lions roosting on either side of what had been the main entrance.

Bollocks, she thought. *Gotta do this. C'mon girl, you can.*

"Don't forget, Titch, you gotta go right inside. All the way down to the basement, take a photo. and email it me," Jake had instructed her, smiling all the time.

As if he's my mate, which he ain't.

Becca knew how to get in; knew exactly where to lift the broken hoardings and slide through; leaving only a sliver of skin off her knee behind.

Once infiltrated in the Adelphi's innards, Becca navigated her way to the Grand Ballroom. Fifty years ago, with its white and black marble floor and wall to wall mirrors, it had been the most glamorous venue in town. Long gone such glamour, now all Becca saw was a rubble-strewn, filthy, echoey space.

Her iPhone bleeped. It was Joss. *Course it is.* "U there yet, girl?"

Becca frowned, but texted back, "Yeah. In ballroom. Stinks."

Joss sent an emoji of a smiley face. "Watch out 4 ded bods."

"Not funny," muttered Becca, but she didn't text the thought back. She didn't have the nerve.

In the shattered spiders' webs of broken mirrors Becca glimpsed movement. Just a brief flicker. Heading for the door. She swung around.

"Who's there?" The glass shards crunched under her trainers. No one replied.

She walked back into the foyer where a trapped sparrow was frantically beating its wings against the ceiling's fabulous plasterwork. *Poor thing, you're stuck like me.* The door leading to the basement was swinging on its hinges. Just as if someone had passed through it a moment ago. Becca gulped. Sweat was already breaking though under her armpits and running down her spine. Knowing she had to go through the swinging door made her sweat more.

Reluctantly Becca pushed against the green baize and, holding her breath because of the musty smell, she inched her way down the stairs. Past signs which read 'Kitchen' and 'Laundry.' Down, down several flights using her iPhone as a torch, until the 'Basement' sign greeted her.

"OK. Let's do this," she tried to encourage herself. Underfoot the carpet was mushy with mould. Some of the spores stuck to her trainers. The walls were splattered with green mouldy patches, which reminded her of a Pollock painting she'd seen in a book.

Worst of all Becca could feel an energy down here, a thrumming. It made her skin itch and the hairs on her arms stand up. Pushing open another swing door she found herself staring at a room filled with floor to ceiling racks once used for storage.

At last she'd arrived at her destination. The basement. The bowel of the beast.

She could hear the skittering feet of rats. Inhaling, the air smelt of a blend of wood, damp and something metallic, which caught at the back of her throat.

"Just rats, that's all, girl. Chill." She tried to breathe steadily, to calm herself. But her heart banged at a quicker rhythm telling her something was wrong.

She knew if she didn't get the pic, she'd be out, ostracised, tormented, laughed at. Right now, though, Becca thought perhaps she could cope with that. Maybe being 'in' wasn't so big a deal.

Facing the racks Becca held up her iPhone at face height and took the shot. In the momentary glare of the flash she glimpsed a figure hanging from one of the top racks, its feet jerking, doing what she knew was called 'the death dance.' She'd learned that off a Netflix history channel documentary. She saw legions of shadowy creatures scuttling around on the ground, busy feeding. She spied a stain creeping out from under the racks, dark and viscous. The air buzzed and hummed; she tasted iron in her mouth.

Becca turned and raced for the stairs. Heart thumping, bile in her throat, sweat pouring down her body. She had only one thought, to get out of there. What if those creatures followed her? What if?

She slipped on the mouldy carpet, fell face down and tasted the dirt. She heaved herself up. In her haste to escape she ripped her hand on the barbed wire fence. She'd have to go to A&E with that tomorrow. It looked deep it. *Damn it!*

Only when she was back on her own street did she pause and take out her iPhone to check the image she'd snapped. Surrounded by her neighbours' bins, gardens and under the streetlamps she now felt calmer.

The image she'd clicked and sent to Joss and Jake revealed only a cellar filled with tall wooden racks stretching back into darkness. There was no hanging man, no scuttling insects, no pool of… fluid. She swallowed at the memory.

Except when Becca peered at the top right corner of the screen she noticed a black blot, like a fly. Or a spore. Or something. She rubbed the screen. It was still there.

Hearing a noise behind her Becca jerked around. No one was there. Except she couldn't help but think she'd just missed seeing something scuttle away, out of sight behind Number 33's recycling bins.

A rat, that's all it is. Lots of them round here.

Letting herself in quietly at the back-door Becca made her plans. First up a shower. Her clothes and skin felt disgusting. Those mould spores had transferred to her. Tomorrow she'd go to A&E, ask for a tetanus shot, make up some story about how she did it. Then she'd find Joss and Jake and tell them to their faces to count her out. Scary as those two made themselves out to be they weren't half as frightening as what she had glimpsed in the guts of The Adelphi.

"Sorted then," she muttered. "I'm all sorted."

Rubbing her arms, she headed for the bathroom. She itched all over, and as she stripped off her clothes the spores floated into the air. *Disgusting. I feel gross.*

Outside her bedroom window a black shape gripped at the drainpipe and slithered up inside the tubing. Sucking in the damp and moist debris inside, it clambered up, lured by Becca's scent. It had followed her trail of skin fragments, blood and sweat from the cellar to her house. It might be blind, but its other senses were overly developed.

It had been alone a long time, waiting, but now it had a new home. A new host. Even now she was breathing in its debris, which was lining her lungs, preparing her for what was to come.

PAIN
Mark Reece

The pain started one Monday morning, waking Paul a few minutes before his alarm clock went off. His left leg felt as if it was made out of stone, but when he tentatively checked himself, there were no cuts. He could not remember his dreams, but whatever they were had made him feel as if he had just moved very quickly. He was out of breath and looked around to see the dim outline of the headboard. When he pulled the bedsheet away, his leg spasmed.

"Uw."

His expression was high pitched and spontaneous, sounding ridiculous enough that he would have burst out laughing had the pain not been so severe. It felt as if something had become wedged between the top of his leg and his hip and was scraping across the joint on his every move. His alarm blared, reverberating through his senses and squeezing his guts.

His every movement was laboured, and activities that he usually carried out without thinking, such as brushing his teeth, turned into awkward manoeuvres where he had to test his limbs and digits to find a position he could bear to hold for a few minutes.

When Paul opened his car door, he put his leg through without thinking before closing his eyes to grimace. Manoeuvring it under the steering wheel was like smiling through a perverse practical joke where someone has sown pins inside one's trousers. He sat still for a few seconds before releasing his breath.

When he reached the office car park, his leg dipped on his every step. People who had arrived after him walked past and out of eyesight very quickly. Paul felt a disturbing sense of loss that went far beyond the inconvenience; he always walked quickly and never complained. *Does this mean I'm disabled?* When he tried to run, he slipped and hopped on his right foot three times, only just stopping himself from falling. After that point, he limited himself to a faltering gait.

Taking the single step into the building was agony, so when Paul reached the lobby, he waited for the lift rather than risk the stairs, hoping not to see anyone he knew.

He stumbled as he entered the office then scanned the room. No one acknowledged his presence until Tom, who sat opposite him, said: "Wet the bed?"

Paul leant down one way then the other to find a muscle that would accept him lowering himself enough to switch his computer on. By the time he had pulled himself back up, his hand having turned white by how hard he had gripped the desk, he was confronted by Tom's grinning face.

"Wet the bed?"

Paul surreptitiously brought a hand to his face to find that his chin was cold. His skin was waxy. In his confusion, he could not understand the words his colleague had used so often before.

"What? What was that?"

Tom rolled his eyes. "You're late. I'm asking you why you're late. Hello. Have you really wet the bed? Or… did you get up to something filthy last night? Was it your birthday? Did your best friend hire strippers for you? That's why you're late, isn't it? I knew it, I knew something was wrong."

Tom looked at the ceiling and laughed good humouredly, which sounded like a roll of thunder. He had only worked in the office for six months – it was his first full time job – and his natural confidence had shone through very quickly. His prominent jaw and thick arms – he always wore a short sleeve shirt, whatever the weather – made his presence there seem incongruous.

"Morning, how are you?"

"Come on, you don't get out of it that easily. You're a creature of habit, I can't remember the last time you didn't get here at five minutes to nine. Twenty past? You're not telling me nothing's going on."

Paul saw that people were starting to pay attention to them. Tom's voice had the booming intonation of the young and assertive.

"I hurt my leg this morning."

"In the orgy arranged for your birthday?"

"I don't know what happened. I must have slept funny because it was like it when I woke up. It feels like I've been shot, I've been hobbling all morning."

"Something similar happened to my friend. There's a department that arranges that kind of thing. It took him ages to sort it out."

Paul was so relieved that Tom had stopped shouting – his voice had sudden taken on a gentle, reflective tone – that he did not realise how strange his words were for several seconds. He peered at the man around his computer, to see that he was now typing in the detached, ponderous way that was his want, frowning, one hand stroking his chin, his fingers jerky as if he was compulsively tapping. If he had been joking then he would have reacted by now. Tom's humour was never subtle, nor could he contain himself if there was any opportunity to laugh. Paul concentrated on his work, which was enough to make him forget.

The pain was much improved by the time he got home, and he only limped every third or fourth step. By reaching down on his right side, he was able to put the plug in the bath, pick up his slippers, and do anything else he wanted. He could continue with the daily carousel.

That gradual improvement continued each day until the weekend, when Paul woke early on Saturday and swiped with both hands, as if trying to fight off multiple assailants. He did not usually wake from nightmares, and the remembrance of the incident earlier in the week filled him with cold fear. He pressed down on the sheet to get into a more comfortable position, and the pain in his elbow was so immediate and acute that he screamed and collapsed on his side, his eyes tightly scrunched.

He took some time to gain the courage to try to sit up, the remembrance of the sensation having scarred his nerves as severely as if his eyes had been burnt. He lifted his pyjama sleeve to find that there were no marks on his skin. He rested against the headboard, feeling it dig into the wallpaper.

There was nothing wrong with his elbow when he dug fingers into it, but when he bent it backwards more than a millimetre, his arm seized up with such violence that Paul was compelled to hold his breath. He lay the limb on the bed as if it was a foreign object. He pulled the bedsheet over himself with his good hand then rested in that position as if he had been stabbed and was waiting to die.

As he drove to work the following Monday, his left hand resting on his lap, Paul remembered Tom's words. Asking him about a previous conversation was fraught with danger. If it had been a joke then it would be repeated ad nauseam. If it had been serious, he would face a more serious problem: Tom was not a person to trust with personal information.

Paul worked silently that morning until most people had gone to lunch. He sat back on his chair and frowned at his screen.

"What's that department called then? The one that causes pain."

"Sorry?"

Paul must have broken his concentration, as he very rarely used the word 'sorry'.

"I was just asking whether you knew what the department that causes pain is called."

"Erm…" Tom rocked on the back legs of his chair and sucked his little finger, and Paul thought that he was going to burst out laughing. "I don't know. Hang on, it's… no, that's just for overtime. Why?"

Now, his attention was wholly focused on Paul, and he narrowed his eyes with a simple man's suspicion.

"I was interested in what you said. Because I've worked here for years and I've never heard anything like that. I was surprised, I suppose. I'd have imagined that something like that would have been more widely advertised."

"Advertised?"

"Maybe that's the wrong word. I mean, that more people would know about it. Because presumably, they'd be part of HR. To punish people, I mean. As part of disciplinary, or…"

"You've lost me. Why would it have to do with disciplinary?"

Paul could not look away and reached out blindly for his water. He was still unsure whether Tom was making fun of him. His mouth was pursed, which usually denoted confusion.

"No particular reason, I just guessed that it would fall under that… type of job. Why do you know about it?"

"Erm… can't say really, just general knowledge. Hang on, I've just remembered something."

Tom tore a piece of notepaper from a pad, screw it into a ball, and threw it at him, making him jerk his head back violently. His booming laughter made everyone in the office look up. Paul hit his elbow against the desk, producing sparks of pain that made his arm feel as if it had been struck by a spiked club. Curiously, despite that he had become the centre of attention, no one who looked at him could tell the difference between a pretended smile, and a pretended smile half smothered by a grimace of pain.

That afternoon, he told Tom that he had to go to a meeting, which produced a half nod in reply. Paul looked over at him a moment, but he gave no indication of having linked that event to their earlier conversation.

He walked out the office and took the lift to the third floor, still not trusting his leg to the stairs. Although it had continued to improve, he felt a twinge every so often if he forgot to take precautions.

The third floor had been abandoned since last year, when building work had started. There had been announcements over the company's Intranet system, and various team meetings had been held where the changes had been 'starbursted', that is, the workers had been told the news. Apparently, cupboards, walls, wooden flooring, and extension leads (the big four) were inefficient and were going to be removed wherever possible. Not only did they take up excessive space (as Paul had been informed during the starburst), but they operated against good working practices in other ways.

For example, cupboards encouraged people to hide their paperwork, rather than sharing ideas across teams. And that was only their most obvious pitfall. The third floor was going to serve as a test site for the new 'perceptive working'.

When Paul got out the lift, he ducked under a metal pole that hung at a forty-five-degree angle from the wall. No building work had taken place for six months following a contractual dispute. The way to his left was entirely blocked by piles of wood. Sawdust flew into the air on his every step, sprinkling on his shirt sleeves like fluttering snow. The carpet had been torn up in places, exposing the concrete. He stopped whenever the ground creaked, as if imagining that he had stood on a landmine. There were windows at regular points along the top of the walls, but they were smeared with debris, casting a filtered light through the air, like the last of a desert sun.

After many cautious steps, Paul reached a door half hidden by a scaffold. He knocked gingerly. There had long been rumours of strange goings-on on the third floor – secret meetings, hidden files – it had even gained a reputation as a place for illicit lovers. Paul was relieved when going inside to find it empty.

Patches of the carpet had been torn up, presumably where power points had been, and there was a pile of landlines in one corner. Otherwise, the room was featureless but for the omnipresent dust, which shimmered on his steps as if thousands of insects watched his every move. Paul rubbed his cheeks. He could not help but be nervous; in a way, *he* was now part of the third-floor legend. He slowly bent down, grimacing when feeling his knee crack.

Paul checked many landlines before finding one with a ring tone. He dialled the number for human resources and grimaced as he tried to find a comfortable position to sit.

He waited for a long time. Paul shuffled repeatedly, staring into the distance. Any surroundings become surreal when one has no alternative but to watch with dead eyes. He could sense that he would have to sneeze soon as more and more dust settled in his nose. The dialling tone buzzed in his ear. Cords wrapped under and around and through the landlines like the tendrils of dead creatures.

"Hello, HR."

The woman held the 'R', making her sound peevish. Despite how long he had waited, Paul suddenly realised that he did not quite know what he wanted. He felt very foolish.

"I'm going to hang up if no one answers."

"Hello, sorry, I had you on speakerphone there. Can you hear me?"

"Yes, this is the HR switchboard, how can I help you?"

Her syllables were crisp now.

"Hello. I'm not sure who I should speak to, but I've been advised to ring this number. I've been having a few problems recently, a few medical problems, and I needed to be put through to the right department. What I mean is, I've been having pain in—"

"Sorry to interrupt, but if you need time off for hospital appointments then you need to talk to your line manager. This is the switchboard for central HR functions."

"No, no, it's not that. You see, it's the pain that's the problem, and I understand that... I wanted to speak to someone who—"

"Oh, I see what you mean. About who's been handling your case, who can give advice, things like that?"

"Yeah."

Paul relaxed for the first time since reaching the floor. He was relieved that the woman knew what he was talking about and that she was able to explain it to him.

"I don't think they take phone calls but let me just check. Hold the line please."

The line started bleeping before he could reply, and Paul found himself staring at the pile of landlines again. While he had been talking, the world around him had faded into nothingness, and he seemed to be sitting in a vacuum. Static was even more abrasive in his ear than the ringing had been, and Paul was relieved when the voice returned.

"Hello, sorry for the wait. I was right, they don't take phone calls."

"How can they not have a phone?"

Paul's voice was curter than he had intended, and the woman was equally cutting in reply: "I didn't say that they didn't have a phone. I said that they don't take phone calls."

"How am I supposed to contact them then?"

Their mutual bad temperedness was cumulative.

"The same as any request, I'll raise a job number and they'll get in contact when they've got time. What's your name please?"

"Paul England."

"Okay... right, I've found you then, Paul. Are you still working on the second floor?"

"I am, but do you mind if I give you my mobile?"

"Is there something wrong with your landline? Because they'll need to prove who they're talking to."

"No, it's fine. It's just that I'd prefer not to talk about this kind of thing in the office."

"That's something you'll need to talk over with them. I can't put your mobile in here though, because if they ring it they could be talking to anyone. It's private information. Data protection."

"Thanks for your help then, can I just ask one other thing before you go?" Paul's voice was suddenly plaintive, offering an unspoken apology for his earlier tone.

"Of course, you can."

"What is this department? It's just that I'd not heard of it until someone in the office said. I'm not sure what to ask when they ring."

Paul's voice trailed off lamely, and he felt desperate that he was asking her for help. However, she was clearly astute, whoever she was, and not bereft of kindness, as after a short pause, she responded in a gentler voice: "They've just been reorganised. They're known as people development now. Mention that when they ring because they don't like people calling them by their old name. You'll be fine. Everything seems intimidating when you do it for the first time. Just don't expect them to be in touch straight away. I know they've got a long waiting list at the moment."

"Okay, well... thanks for your help then."

"I'm sending you your reference number through now. Have a good evening, Paul."

Her final comment was spoken in the professional monotone she had adopted at the start of the conversation. Paul stared at the landlines awhile before replacing the receiver.

He received an e-mail the following afternoon, at which point, Paul was unsure whether he had made the call himself or watched a video of someone else doing so.

"Thank you for your enquiry. Your interest has been

logged. Your reference number is 60YZ-812-13. Please quote this reference number during any discussion of your enquiry. Your adviser today was Sue.

Corporate HR"

Paul tore off a strip of notepaper, wrote down the reference, and placed it in his wallet. He had had a constant dull headache since ringing the number. It was not as painful as his other problems. In fact, it would have barely been noticeable except for the fact that Paul very rarely had headaches. It felt as if stones were being ground against the inside of his skull, chipping off pieces of bone.

For the following week, Paul lived with the maladies in his arm, leg, and head, each of which became more or less severe seemingly at random. Some mornings, he could hardly get out of bed because his leg was rigid and numb. It would be better by night, before his headache mysteriously returned. The pain would be acute for a few seconds, but after he had shuffled and massaged his temples, it became merely drubbing, nagging, wearying. Sometimes, even meeting friends and eating ice-cream seem repetitive and have a flavourless quality. That was the position Paul found himself in.

The sensations had become so integrated into his life that when his landline rung one office afternoon, he had almost forgotten about his outstanding enquiry. Although he had marked the HR e-mail as 'unread' to remind him that they should get back to him, he had received so many subsequent messages that he would have had to scroll down to see it.

"Hello?"

"Who am I speaking to please?"

"It's Paul, from training."

"Oh, *hello*, Paul, I'm Lou, from corporate HR? Hi. I was just getting back to you about your request from the other day. Is this a good time?"

Paul clutched the receiver to his chin and looked around the room furtively. Saying that he would take the call in another room would only make him seem more suspicious. He ducked down and softened his voice, thinking that he must look absurd but not knowing what else to do.

"Yeah, go on."

"I'm *so sorry* about the delay, we've had *loads* of calls recently. It's the time of year. Lots of problems around the summer holidays. Must be a full moon coming up!" Paul chuckled perfunctorily. "Anyway, I was looking through your request this morning and I was a bit confused by it, to be honest. Do you mind explaining in a bit more detail what you need?"

"You don't understand it?"

"It might be how it's written. It is hard for people to write a summary sometimes when they're listening to someone. Instead of reading back what you said, would you just mind telling me the problem again, and hopefully I'll be able to sort it out here and now?"

Paul sat back in his chair and sucked his top lip. No one seemed to be paying any attention to him and he felt annoyed with himself. *Why would the others be interested?* However, he knew that they were. Tom especially. He spoke in a throaty whisper: "Basically, I've been having a number of problems recently with different things. Medical problems. I won't go through it all now, but... they're quite uncomfortable. Anyway, one of my colleagues recommended that I check with you, because I understand that there's part of your department, People Development? That might have something to do with the... issues."

"Yeah, yeah..."

She typed and hummed as he spoke. Whatever 'Lou' thought about the situation, she remained entirely cheerful.

"So, I mean, I'm not sure whether what he was saying can be true. It did sound ridiculous. But I just wanted to confirm whether he was joking with me. If he is, then fine, but if it is true, I wanted to know the best person to speak to to sort things out."

Lou continued to type for some time after he had finished speaking.

"Okay, thanks! I think the original report did get most things right. But I'm still a little... So, in a word, what would you like me to actually help you with today?"

She thinks this is a practical joke, Paul thought. He peered around the computer, but if Tom was listening, he was doing a good job of looking disinterested. He had never shown that much discipline before.

"Well... the first thing is, can you tell me whether my friend was right about the department? Is it real in the way he described it?"

"Your friend sounds lovely, but I can't say whether he's right or wrong without knowing *exactly* what he said. But the way you've described things is basically right."

Paul started to make notes on scrap paper, thinking that they should have equality of reference should the conversation ever be questioned. He paused to read what he had written then looked into the air, trying to remember her exact words. Paul realised that his entire strategy, his entire anger, had been based around the thought that the department would try to hide what it was doing. Now, he realised her confusion; *what do I want?*

"Right. Is there anyone I can speak to about it? I'd like to ask about my file if I can, what decisions have been made about me, whether I can appeal them, things like that."

"I'll have a look. One moment please."

She was gone before he could say anything. He watched minutes tick past on the screen clock. The office was unnaturally quiet.

"Hello!"

"Hi."

"The best thing you can do is arrange a meeting. It might not be for a while, but if you've got lots of questions then that might be easier than trying to work things out over the phone."

"Erm... okay."

He heard typing again. Paul held the receiver as tightly against his ear as he could and heard too many keys being pressed for it to be just 'Lou'. It sounded like a whole room full of people.

"Okay, how about... the twentieth, is that convenient for you?"

That was three weeks on Friday. As Paul looked over his diary, he saw that he had booked leave on that day. However, he had only planned to do a little decorating. He had anticipated waiting months and was not going to risk anything by asking for another date.

"That's fine, do you want me to...?"

"I'll send you one of those e-mail invitation thingies. That's lovely. Beautiful. Okay, is there anything else I can help you with today?"

"No, that's great. Thanks for your help, Lou."

"You're welcome. Bye bye then."

She hung up before he could say 'bye' himself.

The following morning, Paul's pillow was red when he woke. He spluttered, not recognising the coppery smell for a few seconds.

When he went to the bathroom, he saw that his left nostril was engorged with blood, as if he had been punched. He threw up in the sink.

Paul had thought that the three-week deadline would put his mind at ease and give him a goal to focus on. Instead, the intervening time was a misery. The various pains lost their distinctiveness, merging into monotone aches. In a strange way, he missed the unique sensations – the stumble induced by the pulled muscle, the woozy stagger induced by a nose bleed, the grinding sensation in his elbow that he could almost hear, as if someone was sawing through the bone. Now, those old friends were barely distinguishable from ennui.

He only checked where he needed to go on the afternoon before his appointment, the event having become abstract after being arranged. When he opened the entry within his e-mails, he was surprised to see that it was going to be held at somewhere called 'Everidge Memorial Centre'. Paul looked up the address on the Internet, but after zooming into various maps, he could not find anything that looked like an office. The area was in a suburb some distance from the city centre, and he had not known that the company had any buildings there.

He was in a curious state of mind the following morning, waiting for his alarm to go off before jumping out of bed and rushing to get ready, then slowing down, not wanting to get there early. However, he then thought that because he did not know where he was going, it would be best to leave as soon as possible, so he hurried out the house, zipping up his coat as he went.

His sat-nav told him that he had reached his destination when he turned into a thoroughfare road with a school in the distance, a brook to his right, and residential streets to his left. When he drove into one of them, the device insisted that he turn back. Paul parked outside a house with a hole in its front wall, thinking that he would not forget where he had left the car.

He walked to the end of the street and rested against the wire fence that separated the school from the road. There was no sign of movement, and the chalk markings on the floor indicated that it was a primary school. When he heard footsteps further down the street, he turned and hurried away, aggravating a pain in his neck.

He checked his watch to see that the meeting was due to start in eight minutes. The sun was shining, and when he absently scratched his nose, Paul realised that he was sweating. He sat on the side of the brook, thinking that at least he was wasting work time rather than his own.

The bank leading to the water was very steep. Paul was struck with reverie at the thought of how his life had led to that point. He scrunched his eyes as a wasp flew towards him and was convulsed by a coughing fit, each rasp like sandpaper against the back of his throat. Paul tried to stand, and his leg seized up, sending him doing forward rolls down the bank.

He dug his nails into the grass, slowing his descent, although landing on his back knocked him breathless. Water flowed through his coat, up his sleeves, and down his trouser legs. Eventually, he got to his feet by a combination of pushing and pulling with various limbs, and water seemed to pour from his fingers.

His shirt was sodden and covered with dirt. Paul shook himself like a dog and his vision fragmented into pieces. There was a cave in one of the banks. He put his arms out to steady himself, and when the blurriness faded, he saw that it was real. In one way, it was hard to believe that the company had an office in such a location, but when he thought about it, it was the most natural place in the world. When Paul took a step towards it, he dipped to one side as if he had sunk into quicksand before recovering his gait.

The space was carved out of the bank with professional smoothness. He could see nothing beyond; it was as black as if a piece of night had fallen from the sky. The moment he stepped through, Paul was in no doubt that he was in the right place. The air was damp and the walls were made out of a cool, hard material that his hands slid off as he went. There was just enough illumination that he could see there was nothing in his way, although not enough that he knew whether or not the corridor was straight.

The further he went, the more blasé Paul became, until he daydreamed as he walked, wondering whether he would be dried out by the time he returned to his car.

When he lost his footing, Paul spun on his back as if skidding through a slide. His stomach tightened when he saw the green bricks in the ceiling. When he tried to grab the sides, he winced at the screech of his nails scraping against a surface as hard as steel.

Paul did not know how much he had screamed, and how much the ringing in his ears was caused by swirling water. He flapped around ineffectually before realising that he had stopped. Paul found himself in some kind of chamber, perhaps the size of his lounge, with black green walls and dome shaped lights on the ceiling that dimly lit the room. There was a solitary pathway leading from the chute he had come from, across the centre of the room, with lapping water either side. It led to a metal stand, on which rested a tablet device held in place by metal spokes. A balding man sat behind it on an uncomfortable looking wooden stool. The only sounds were the light tapping of his fingers against the keys, and water dripping from Paul's shirt to the floor.

The man looked up, smiled, and gestured for him to come over, before returning his attention to the device. Paul followed the path, unsteady on his feet, and when he was by the stand, he kicked something hard and unseen, sharply enough to make him fall to his knees. He pressed his fingers into his shoe, thinking that he had broken his toes, before eventually feeling them wriggle.

"Are you alright, Paul?"

"Yes."

When the man's face came into view, Paul jumped, jolting his ankle.

"Nothing too bad, I hope?"

"No."

Paul knew that he would be fine in a few seconds. However, until that point, he could only speak a single word, lest he gasp with pain.

"It's quite hard to see, I'm afraid. Have a seat."

He gestured to a space behind the plinth. Paul squatted and tried the area with his hands, to find that it was damp and covered with grainy dirt. However, the man did not seem to mind, so nor could he. He wore old fashioned glasses with string dangling behind his ears, and had thick eyebrows with stray hairs sticking out. His skin was pitted and his collar was far too large for his neck, making him look like a giant bird.

"George. Nice to meet you."

It felt strange shaking hands sitting down.

"Now, I've discussed your enquiry with my colleagues and it's a bit confusing, but I think I understand. Are you okay there?" The man leant over and touched his shoulder kindly.

"Still a bit sore. George, why have I been asked to come here?"

The man lowered his voice. "I'll be honest with you, Paul. I think it's purely because it's awkward to get to so that people don't bother. I know it's annoying, but I hope you realise that it's nothing to do with my team. We know how it is for people, we've got to go through the same process ourselves." He leant back and spoke at a normal volume. "So, did you just want to confirm what's going to happen next, that kind of thing?"

"Kind of… is it your department that's caused the pain over the last few months?"

"Well… we put the procedures in place. Obviously it wasn't our decision."

"Okay, is this part of some disciplinary, or…?"

"No, you've got a good record as far as I know. Do you want me to check? I can access the electronic records now. Not all the files have been transferred over, but I doubt there's anything on the paper files that you need to worry about. They'll relate to things years ago."

"Right…"

George nodded and gave a small smile as he waited for Paul to express his meaning, as if encouraging a child to say their first word. "I think this has been the confusion from the start. Why would this be happening if you've not done anything wrong?" George laughed then held up a hand apologetically. "Paul, I don't know whether you missed a day at school, but… you must be under a lot of stress, the reorganisation has affected a lot of people. It's easy to forget about all this…" George gestured at the ceiling. "This is paid employment. I do appreciate that when you're concentrating on your work, the… nature of things gets lost sometimes. In short, the organisation has to extract its rights, otherwise it wouldn't remain competitive. Look, I'm going to give you something to read on your way back. I suggest you ring your manager tonight and book next week off. It's not helping anyone for you to be going around like this."

"But my legs are—"

"You'll be surprised how much clearer things are by tomorrow."

George stood and handed him a leaflet, and Paul climbed to his feet. It had a cartoon of a man at a computer, above the words: 'practical tips to reduce workplace stress', written in loopy letters.

"It might not seem like it, but it will have done you some good coming here today. A flash of reality is good for you. Not too much. Just a flash."

Suddenly, Paul wanted nothing more than to leave. "Is it…?"

He pointed in the direction of the slide he had taken to get there, before wondering whether the man would be able to see him.

"No, no, the water only flows one way."

Paul took a step in the direction he indicated. George smiled down at him, his cheeks creasing with care. "You're a good lad, Paul. Don't let things get to you." He leant back and smiled wryly. "The processes shouldn't be too impersonal. As long as I'm here, we'll do things the traditional way."

He plucked the leaflet out of Paul's hands, folded it, and put it in his shirt pocket. He smiled, patted him on the shoulder, then punched him in the nose with a movement so sudden that he was careering through another tunnel before realising what had happened.

When he went around a bend, he felt a trouser leg catch on an outcropping. The speed of the water was enough to tear him away, and the sound of the material ripping reverberated through his mind. Just as he was getting used to wet ears, he felt himself fly through the air and land on a patch of grass with a bump. He wiped a hand across his face, smearing blood, before looking down to see that his clothes had been shredded.

He opened the leaflet to find that the words inside were written in large type, with colourful illustrations that gave the document the air of advertising. The first section was headed: 'effective lifestyle management'. Paul carefully folded it into his rags. He wandered through the street, bleeding, naked, and alone, trying to remember where he had parked.

THIS LITTLE PIGGY
Teika Marija Smits

My mother once told me that Sartre was right. "You know, about hell. And people. How it's created by those around us." But then I remember her sighing and shaking her head. "No, that's not quite true. Hell comes from within."

She pulled her long cardigan tighter about her and then put her hand to her forehead. "The mind. The body. They're linked, of course."

I knew she'd been seriously ill years earlier, before I'd been born, and so I assumed that she was referring to her illness. But shortly after I told her that Lizzie and I would be starting on IVF – I must've said something like *It's going to be hell* – she turned on me.

"Hell!" she hissed. "You've got to be joking, right? You're lucky to have that as an option. Don't go complaining about it. Can you even imagine what life was like for infertile women before IVF came along? Because *that* was hell. And believe me, I'm an expert on that."

Years of resentment clawed at my throat. "Well, go on, Mum," I said, my voice tight. "Share some of your expertise. Because I'm sick of the selfless martyr act. And why is it that Lizzie can't do anything right by you?"

"This isn't about Lizzie!"

"Really?"

"Really."

Suddenly, her shoulders slumped, and she took a wobbly step towards the kitchen table. I helped her into a chair.

231

"Do you really want to know about hell? My hell?" she asked.

"Yes," I said, angrily. "I do."

She looked at me with searching eyes, her frown lines deep, accusatory.

She began to toy with the gold cross on her necklace. "There've been so many times I wanted to tell you, but..."

"Go on, Mum," I said, more gently this time.

She took a deep breath. "There was this article, you see. In a woman's magazine. It must've been sometime in 1976. Two years before the first IVF baby was born. It was about the lengths some women would go to, to get pregnant. One woman had become fixated on visiting so-called 'fertile' places, you know, pagan sites. She and her husband would make love amongst standing stones and on chalk downs where ancient tribes had carved men and women, their sexual organs huge, swollen. After two years of this she finally became pregnant.

"Another woman pushed her body to all kinds of extremes, going on drastic diets and gruelling exercise regimes to make her body 'perfect'. She'd eat all kinds of strange things, like coal, caviar, raw meat, cough syrup – anything that was thought to maybe enhance fertility. 'I went through hell to get my baby,' I remember her saying. 'But it was worth it.'

"I cut out the article and carried it around with me. I felt as though these women understood me. They knew about *the emptiness*. And the desperate, desperate urge, no *hunger* to have a baby.

"The word 'hell' kept going round my head. Was I prepared to go through hell to have a baby? And that's when it struck me. Hell was a house. Specifically, the old Gascoigne house, down by the river Skerne."

An image of a mouldering Victorian mansion came into my mind. Along with some myth about women luring men to the river, to their deaths. "I think I remember it. Wasn't it turned into luxury flats?"

"Yes, but back then it was this decrepit old building. Ivy was choking it to death, the windows were broken, paint was flaking off the walls and it was full of rubbish. A slum."

"You went inside?" I said, confused.

"Twice. The first time was when it was up for auction. Your dad, bless his soul, had this idea that we'd maybe do up the old place. Turn it into a fancy hotel. His job with the American firm was paying him good money. He said it could be a fun project for me.

"But before the auction, when we viewed it with some other people, I just remember feeling very frightened. There was something about the place, I mean, besides the rubble, broken glass, and what remained of the battered furniture, there was – how can I put it? – an atmosphere. Like there was something malicious about the place. I remember a man whispering to his wife that the place used to belong to a doctor. But that he can't have been a very good one, because all his kids got sick and died.

"The estate agent was trying his best to stay enthusiastic, but when we came across a room that had 'This is Hell' written on its door in red spray paint even he went silent."

A single tear rolled down my mother's face. I put out my hand but she didn't take it. Instead, she took a handkerchief from her pocket and dabbed at her eyes.

"Well, of course, Colin and I weren't interested in a place that was being used as the neighbourhood drug den, or whatever, so we never went to the auction. But after I read that article, I finally understood what I had to do. I had to spend a week in that house."

"What?" I said, incredulous.

"I wish I could say that it wasn't that bad. But it was. It was the worst week of my life. And the number of times I've wished I could unmake that stupid, stupid decision. Well…"

She sniffed again, her eyes wet with tears.

"So what happened?"

She shrugged. "It's funny, isn't it? The things an old woman remembers. I can still recall debating with myself about whether I should allow myself any food. A blanket. Some toilet paper. After all, should one prepare for hell? Wasn't that cheating? In the end I went empty-handed. Colin had just gone down to London for the week, so I knew he wouldn't miss me. He'd only ever phone the once, when he arrived, and I left a note for my neighbour saying that I'd be away at an old friend's. Which was kind of true. It would be just me and my old friend, the emptiness. Anyway…" She paused, suddenly lost in thought, and then took another deep breath.

"So, late that September night I walked along the river, found a way through the brambles, and there I was. It was easy enough to get into the place since the back door was rotten through, but when I was inside, I had my first fright. Rats. Scrabbling and skittering all about the ground floor. I nearly turned back there and then. I wish I had."

I held out my hand again. This time she took it.

"But I persevered. I forced myself through the dark and went upstairs to make my 'camp' in one of the smaller bedrooms. I remember lying down on a filthy mattress, looking up at the moon and thinking about my own bed at home. The mattress was white – or rather, it had once been white – with blue stripes. There was dust everywhere; whenever I moved, dust would swirl into the air and settle on my hair, get into my lungs. I cursed myself for not bringing any water. And that's how I got through the first night – with the promise that if I didn't find any drinking water the next day I would go home.

"But the following day, one of the outdoor taps sputtered into life. The water was filled with grey flakes. But it was drinkable. So I had to stay."

"Mum," I began, squeezing her hand. She ignored me.

"The days were okay. I'd walk out to the orchard, enjoy the dust-free air, and eat apples and blackberries.

"But the nights... I hardly slept of course. Every noise was a 'something' coming to get me. And when I did sleep, strange dreams, full of the murderous doctor and his dead babies, haunted me."

More tears rolled down her cheeks.

"But that was nothing to the horror of the last night I spent there.

"Because on the last night – it was a Friday – there was a noise to be properly scared of. Because it was a human noise.

"At first, there were voices outside, then the creaking of the backdoor. The sound of rats scarpering. Bottles clinking. A tape recorder playing a tinny pop song.

"I froze. The door to my room was half open. If anyone were to pass by I'd be seen. So slowly, and ever so quietly, with my heart beating so hard I thought it would burst, I crept to the wardrobe in the corner of the room and crawled inside. I curled myself into a ball and covered my ears with my hands. But it wasn't enough to muffle the sound I wish I could erase from my memory. A woman's scream.

"Panic, and fear, drove me deeper into the wardrobe, and myself.

"I kept saying the Lord's Prayer over and over, breathless, tears squeezing themselves out of my eyes. Urine seeping through my trousers.

"Hours must've passed. And, somehow, out of the delirium I had retreated to I re-emerged. Daylight streamed through the cracks in the wardrobe, and when I uncovered my ears there was silence. I was so relieved I began to cry all over again.

"Eventually, I ventured down, alert to every noise. But the house was empty. As I made for the back door – fresh litter, beer cans and empty syringes amidst the rubble – I suddenly paused. Escape was only a few metres away, but my gut twisted and wouldn't let me go any further. What if there *was* someone there? In the room with the red writing on the door? And they needed help? But I couldn't do it. I couldn't make myself look, and so instead, I ran. Just like the littlest pig – *'wee wee wee' all the way home*. And I never spoke to anyone about it. Ever."

She sniffed and then dried her eyes. She looked at me, a sad smile on her face, and then gave my hand a squeeze. "So now you know. And everything else that happened to me in the next year was like nothing, compared to the remorse that I felt, and which poisoned my every waking thought. Why hadn't I been brave enough to look in that room?

"Stupidly, I held onto the idea that I'd been through enough to become pregnant. And nine months later, when I began to feel sick and tired, my belly aching and my period all over the place, I just knew that this time, I'd managed to conceive a child.

"It was a while before I went to the GP. Colin came

with me. I remember him looking at me with worried eyes as I happily cradled my stomach.

"He was right to be anxious though, because as it turned out the baby wasn't a baby, but a tumour. And an ugly one at that. Do you know what a teratoma is?"

I shook my head, tears streaming down my face.

"It's a tumour that has bits of other body parts in it. Hair, eyes, teeth. A hand.

"I was lucky though. At least, that's what everyone said. It was removed and I survived."

She let go of my hand and sighed. "All my life I've been selfish. Driven by two urges: to have a baby; to survive. I thought that maybe adopting you would be my first selfless act. When I saw a photo of you in that Romanian orphanage, wearing a babygro the colour of dust, in a cot with a filthy blue-and-white striped mattress, I thought I could save you. But it turns out I was wrong about that too. Because in the end, my precious boy, you gave me far more than I could ever have given you."

"Mum," I began, suppressing a sob, "don't say that. You did save me. My life as it is now… is all because of you."

I went over to her and simply held her. "I love you, Mum," I said instinctively, my voice breaking. And for the first time in my life I realized that those words were not enough. Yet also too much.

ALSO AVAILABLE

1964 by Franklin Marsh
Derek Edge and the Sun-Spots by Andrew Darlington
Daddy Giggles by Stephen Bacon
Black Sheep by Gary Fry
Jamal Comes Home by Benedict J. Jones
Waiting by Kate Farrell
Lilly Finds a Place to Stay by Charles Black
The Mutant's Cry by David A. Sutton
The Sanitation Solution by Walter Gascoigne
Up and Out of Here by Mark Patrick Lynch
Late Shift by Adrian Cole
The Great Estate by Shaun Avery
Nine Tenths by Jay Eales
Envelopes by Craig Herbertson
Tunnel Vision by Tim Major
Life is Precious by M. J. Wesolowski
Canvey Island Baby by David Turnbull

www.ingramcontent.com/pod-product-compliance
Lightning Source LLC
Chambersburg PA
CBHW052032260626
47163CB00006B/198